SIN-CITY WALKER:
Two of A Kind

Stephen R. Sobotka

ARTWerks Books
United States of America

Cover art by Christi Smith Hayden
Cover & layout design by Stephen R. Sobotka

Published by ARTWerks Books
First Edition June 2007
6232 S. Dale Mabry Hwy., #5
Tampa FL. USA

Written & Edited by
Stephen R. Sobotka

ISBN 978-0-6151-6961-3

Printed in the United States of America

PLEASE NOTE!

The story within may contain subject matter or conent of either a violent or an erotic/sensual nature that some may find objectionable.

This story is intended for mature audiences. If you are under the age of 18 years, then please DO NOT read this book!

-- *S.R.S.*

ACKNOWLEDGEMENTS

To God, for giving me my talent, imagination, and the means to develop them both, and to my Grandmothers -- Norma J. and Beatrice -- for showing me such incredible worlds, which could only be found between the pages of a book ...

To Christine Morgan, For giving me the inspiration to write, and encouraging me to never quit believing and keep on writing stories back in 1995, and to Greg Weisman, for trying to teach me a hard lesson in 1999 — which *finally* sunk in in 2005! — to separate realistic goals from *'bull$#@!'* ...

And to my twin sister, Patricia, my mother Mary and my Father, Stephen Sr., for their love, support and a good kick-in-the-tail once in a while.

See, Dad? I told you I'd make it someday!

A DEDICATION...

To Christi Smith Hayden... For your artwork, constructive critisism, honesty and support for over these past 13 years.

May we always keep sharing the gift of our friendship in the years to come.

hugs! -- Stephen

TWO OF A KIND

1. - Frankie's Bar

Now I need a drink, it's going to be on you
The day of judgment ain't far away
But who'll be the judge, it's hard to say
Mnnn . . . yeah that's hard to say.

— "Dead Man's Blues", Supertramp.

H ey, buddy? "Hey . . . hey you, Buddy!"

Lifting my tired peepers from the dried water spots on the polished oak surface, I peered back at the fat man behind the bar. "Yeah?"

His dark eyes indexed up and down my pale face, before frowning at the trio of empty glasses near my left hand. "You, ah . . . had enough?" From the expression on his kisser, I must've looked like a man who was well on his way to being stone-cold drunk, or dead. Either description would've fit me, far as I was concerned.

"Nah. Set 'em up . . . Joey," I said, reading the nametag pinned to his faded embroidered vest.

Leaning towards me, Joey propped himself

against the edge of the bar and asked, "Are you *sure* you want another one of those, Chum?"

I dropped my chin to my chest to peer at the glasses next to me. "Sure . . . why not?

Joey reached up with a relatively dry corner of a bar towel, knocking a few thin, gray hairs askew as he mopped his balding pate with it. "Why not-?!" He cleared his throat. "Chum, I've been tending bar for over thirteen years, and I ain't seen anyone — I mean anyone! — drink three of my special Bloody Mary's in one sittin', and now you want another one?

"So? S'there a law against me havin' a fourth?"

"Well, no . . . but, c'mon! You're gonna kill yourself if you have another one of those!"

How little he knew of me, I thought.

Tipping the thin-brimmed fedora off of my forehead, I muttered, "Look . . . s'my life, 'kay?" Reaching inside my jacket, I fished out a twenty and slapped it on the bar top. "Set 'em up again."

Shaking his head, Joey reached for the faded bill. "You need to sober up, chum," he said, pushing my money back to me. "I'm sorry-."

"Yeah, well . . . I'm sorry, too." Pulling my alcohol-soaked wits together, I stared into his eyes . . . hard.

His eyes went wide as headlights as he sucked in a sharp breath. He started to step back, only to go slightly slack-faced as I 'pushed' my way into his head. Joey tried to fight back, but he had no real strength of will, really.

"I think," I said, some steel in my voice now, "that you want to give me that drink."

Numbly, Joey nodded his head. "Yeah . . . sure, chum. I . . . wanna, give you, that drink."

I let his mind go slowly, easing back so he wouldn't get really spooked. "Yeah, well, make it snappy with that drink."

Snapping back, Joey blinked, shaking his head as he stared at me. "Geez, um, wha-?"

"Joey, my drink?" I tapped the corner of the twenty, still under his hand. "Bloody Mary, one of your specials, remember?"

Joey looked down briefly, curling his fingers to pull the money into his palm. "Sure." Reaching with his other hand to scoop up my glasses, he said, "Sure thing, buddy."

Leaning back, I looped one arm over the low back of the barstool. "It's a triple."

Joey shrugged, before he turned to waddle towards the other end of the bar. "Your funeral."

"Too late," I said softly. I leaned further back, feeling the wood beneath the padded seat creak as my weight settled on the stool's two back legs. Looking away, I slid my eyes over the rest of this little bar; Frankie's it was called.

From the sputtering neon beer sign behind the rows of glasses behind the bar, to the hip-swaying Elvis clock above the beat-up Wurlitzer jukebox in the far corner, belting out some scratchy blues tune. It was that certain time of the night; where people that came from all over, who didn't want to go to bed or travel anywhere near the glare of the 'main drag' could come in, drink in peace and basically get lost in the black curtain of the night.

Yeah, this was Eastside Vegas at its best. Real poetic, eh? Well, I sort of specialize in that sort of thing. Not poetry, mind you. I mean I'm someone who knows the night pretty intimately... no thanks to a certain little birdie I knew some decades ago.

Hell, I'm getting ahead of myself here. The truth is, while I may look like a thirty-something in a cheap suit and wingtips . . . I'm really a vampire.

I can hear the smart remarks already!

No need to go all gonzo about it. I mean, my life — or un-life, call it as you like it — isn't much to write home about. I mean, what's to tell about the life of a vampire that people already know, eh?

Joey returned to my end of the bar just then; slouching over to put a fresh drink in front of me.

"Here you go, buddy," he said. Even though it was clear a part of him didn't want to give that drink to me, he had no choice really. That mental voodoo I do might not make me a damn Korvac, but when I work the mojo, it pretty much sticks.

"Thanks," I said, pulling the deep-red concoction closer. "Keep the change."

Shrugging, Joey moved off to start cleaning up some of the dirty glasses building up after the last round of drinks had been polished off by the other patrons.

Looking into the mirror behind the bar, I grimaced at myself . . . Oh, sure! I can see myself pretty clearly, since vampires *do* reflect in a mirror. Don't let all that junk about what vampires can or can't do throw you! It's bunk. Pretty much like what a lot of so-called 'experts' have written about vampires in recently.

I whisked the contests of my Bloody Mary around inside the glass, before taking the obligatory celery stalk out and dropping it down onto the paper napkin left there with my drink.

Lifting the glass, I looked once more at myself in the mirror and, giving the glass a tip-salute, I muttered, "Here's to you, John Walker!", before tossing back half of the drink in one gulp. It made a slightly-pleasant burn as it slid down my throat, before pooling in my stomach briefly as it moved along into my bloodstream. Didn't do much to warm me up further, but I still shivered from the sensation.

Lowering the glass, I slipped back into my idle thoughts, tuning out the bar, Joey and everything else. Such was the reality of my life these past few nights. A real pip, eh? Here I am, in Las Vegas; the other 'city that never sleeps', an experience never to be missed in one's lifetime, or so I was told once. After someone at one of my usual late-night card games went on and on about his last trip here, I figured I needed the change in scenery.

I mean, face it, even as one of the living undead, I was practically living in a rut . . . figuratively speaking.

So, I made the arrangements — booked a flight, room and board, along packing the bare essentials — and soon found myself here, smack in the middle of the Nevada desert, among the glitz and bright lights of the Vegas Strip.

To be honest though... after four nights' worth of sights, shows, sounds and such that made up this adult playground, I was bored to death. I mean, this trip was intended to pick up my spirits. To look at me now, you'd see nothing but a worn-down, garbage dump of a thing that was masquerading as a living man. I mean, not to use the obvious pun, folks... but being a vampire sucks.

Complain much, don't I?

It's just that so many people have all the wrong ideas about what it's really like being a vampire! I mean, a lot of writers and such have made this existence out to be something mystical, romantic, erotic and all . . . can you believe that? Back where I grew up, things like vampires were lumped in with the boogey man as something to scare kids into going to bed on time.

Nowadays, the latest generation of kids want to 'live the immortal life of Dracula'! They've created a damned sub-culture; all about people that want to live for the night, drink blood and exist forever.

Malarkey, I tell you! If they really knew what it was like . . . well, let's just say I never had a servant who called me 'Master', for starters!

All my life has ever consisted off was just a regular pattern of dullsville. I get up at the crack of dusk, rise and greet the start of another night of doing my usual business. This usually means I find one of the usual, all-night dives I frequent in my neck of the woods, and spend all hours just drinking and playing cards. Hey, beats working a graveyard shift for some bozo's time clock, believe me . . . but even then, that's just the general state of things.

Once in a while, when I get hungry, I go out to look for a bite . . . that's just shorthand for me finding a local livestock warehouse or barn, where I can get my fill of blood and not call any undue attention. Believe me, it's much safer than hunting for live bodies, or chowing down on some transient or hobo that happens to be passing through! The last thing you ever want to do as a modern-day vampire is leave a string of corpses for someone to find . . . the local law doesn't take too kindly to that kind of thing.

Though, I do admit, no matter how careful I try to be, once in a while I do draw the attention of some whacko, wannabe vampire-hunter that's looking to make a name for themselves! They believe they've got the brass, but more often than not, they're just kooks or some nervous kid that's read too much into that sub-culture I just mentioned.

Usually though, I don't panic when someone comes looking to deal me the ultimate dirt-nap. I give them a few, well-placed 'suggestions' — like I did for Joey over there — and send them on their way.

Other times, a well-placed fist and a few nights in the local Gray-Bar Hotel will dissuade the more dogged and determined ones. It usually keeps them off my backside, leaving the Police to deal with them, so I can melt away into the countryside.

Granted, that sort of thing right now would almost be a welcome distraction to me, as I sit here. Almost, mind you. The last thing I'm certain Vegas needs is a open call to arms over someone getting their ticket punched, thanks to me.

So, there's the hand life dealt me, so to speak; just your modern-day vampire, stuck in the last few days of his Vegas vacation, getting drunk with nothing better to do with myself.

God! If there was any sort of justice in this world, I'd treat myself to a stake and do the world the favor of ever hearing this bloodsucker gripe about his mid-unlife crisis.

The front door to the bar flew open, allowing another barfly to wing in from the glittering lights of the 'Strip outside.

I looked up from where I was racing a pair of pistachio shells over a lake of melted ice water on the bar . . . left after I'd finished most of that last Bloody Mary. Glancing at Elvis on the wall, I saw his long hand hadn't even crossed the middle of his tick-ticking pelvis.

Well, time munches on, eating away at what little life you have left, hm? Getting back to the race, I could hear Joey's voice perk up when the newcomer made their presence known at the bar. "Hey, doll! Good to see you 'round here again!"

"Hey, Joe. Did you miss me?"

That voice managed to pierce through the wall of noise around me. It was alto-low and vel-vet smooth . . . a dame, for certain. No guy could sound like that, far as I was concerned.

"So, what will you have, the usual?" Joey asked, slipping away from the sink to slouch against the bar.

"Actually, I feel like having something tart tonight. Make me a rum punch, please?" the newcomer purred.

"Anything for you doll. I'll fix ya one, right up," Joe said.

I couldn't help the inward chuckle at Joey's expense; the big guy looked more animated than he had all night, as he made the newcomer their drink.

"So, to what do we owe the honor of your appearance so soon? Thought you'd be back East for a while yet." Joey rattled some ice around before plunking a few cubes into the tumbler in front of him.

"Glamour-Con, Joe . . . couldn't miss out on it, you know that."

"Ah, I wondered if you'd be in town for that fashion convention!" Placing her drink on the bar with a clunk of glass and ice, he moved some glasses around as he kept talking. "Had some gals in here the other night . . . talking big business and all."

"Well, a friend of mine's running the fashion show this year and she had a vendor drop out at the last minute," the stranger replied with a lot of self-satisfaction in her voice. "Lucky me, I was right there with the new spring line."

"And opportunity knocked harder than a bill collector on the first of the month, eh?" Joey asked.

'Doll' just chuckled. "I had buyers lined up around the booth before the catwalk was barely cold. I even landed a contract for a major West Coast distributor." Ice clinked in the middle of her pause. "So, with my boss happy, here I am, ready to celebrate."

"If you're in th' mood, doll, you should be hoofin' it up at those ritzy places down on th' Strip," Joey said, even though he had a twist of tease in his tone.

"Well . . . I don't know about that." Another clink of ice against glass. "There's nobody else I know on the Strip that mixes a drink as smooth as you."

"Aw, thanks!"

"So, Joe, how have things been with you?"

Well, this conversation turning into one of those 'catching up' kind of talks, I sighed and tried to tune it out. Wasn't my thing. Eavesdropping, that is. Besides, I'd been hearing snips and sound-bites of dozens of similar exchanges each and every night. I turned back to my own drink, taking another sip of the diluted red mess . . . .

"Hey, would you mind if I sit here?"

That sounded very close. Like at-my-elbow close! Glancing left, I nearly lost what internal balance I had left tonight! I mean, I may be a dead man walking, but some things will always grab a guy's attention and a beautiful woman will do it every time. The woman in question stood there, leaning against the bar with most of her weight on one leg. She must've been no taller than five-eight, with a figure that wasn't too skinny or too plump. Lithe and trim were words that came to my mind. She wore a jacket and skirt in navy blue; the skirt long enough for business, but short enough to show off her incredible legs. The open collar of her gray blouse framing a long stretch of smooth creamy skin visible from her long neck to the swell of her cleavage.

On any other woman, it would have looked conservative, and perhaps just a little old-fashioned. On her . . . well, the sight of it made my teeth start to ache!

"Ahem."

Startled, my eyes shot up and locked onto her face. She was looking back at me from underneath a fringe of red and burnished-gold kissed bangs; her green eyes twinkling like wet gemstones, which only accented the long hair framing her heart-shaped face. "Like the view?" she asked, arching one eyebrow.

I snapped back into my former frame of mind. "Ah, pardon me! I didn't mean to—!"

"Don't worry about it," she chuckled, shaking off my attempted apology with a shake of her head, which made her long red tresses brush against the tops of her shoulders. "I've had guys looking at me all day long," she added with a sigh, perching her behind on a neighboring chair as she crossed her stocking-clad legs with a silken hiss. "Even had a couple swear I look like some Playboy Playmate."

"Don't let her kid you, chum." Joey said to me, as he brought her a chaser. "She enjoys the attention."

"Well, that is true," she admitted, grinning good-naturedly at Joey as she nodded her thanks for the drink. "It's just part of my job." Taking a sip, she regarded me over the rim of the glass, her eyes twinkling like amber jewels. "After all, as my dear old Aunt used say . . . 'there's nothing wrong with showing the world what you have.'. If it helps to generate a little random pleasure for others and yourself, it's good for you."

I shrugged my shoulders, shifting so I wasn't completely facing away from her. "If you say so, Miss-?"

"Maxine Reynolds, from the New Haven branch of my family . . . not that they'd ever admit it. I'm the 'black sheep' of the flock, you see." Pausing to sip her drink, she continued. "That's because I actually work for a living, as opposed to hanging around the country club and letting the chinless wonders of high society drool over me. I didn't get your name, Mister-?"

"Name's . . . just call me Bud." No way was I going to tell a stranger my real name.

"Bud?" she blinked, disbelief visible on her face. "You do realize that if you say your last name is Weiser, I'll have to hurt you, don't you?"

I felt a smirk trying to curl around the left

side of my lips, but I quashed it before it got away from me. "Actually, it's Walker. You know . . . like the whiskey, but don't call me 'Blackie' or 'Red' either.

Maxine's expression turned thoughtful. "Walker . . . hm, Walker." She sounded like she was rolling my name around on her tongue, like sampling a dose of a fine liqueur. "Funny, that name sounds familiar, somehow." Shaking her head, she added, "Oh well. I'll figure it out. I do enjoy a challenge. Since you're taking some pains to hide your full name."

I shrugged, turning my glass around with one hand. "Persons can't be too careful with their names these days, y'know . . . ?"

"Well, being careful is one thing," Maxine admitted. "In any case, 'Bud' will do. For now." She leaned against the bar, letting her glass drift to the bar top with a less-audible clink. Her finger started to trace the edge of the rim, making the light glint off of its long red fingernail.

"So, Bud, what brings you here to Vegas, business or pleasure?" Her eyes danced. "Perhaps a little of both?"

This wasn't the sort of conversation I was expecting. Setting my gaze back down on my glass, noting absently that it was nearly empty, I stated, "No real reason."

"Really." Her reply was more like she only partially accepted the face value of my answer, not a query for confirmation.

I hoped she wasn't the sort to pry. I just wanted to just end this conversation and go back to being miserable . . . and yet, there was a small part of me that was beginning to enjoy her presence. Despite that, I just shrugged again. "Yeah, really."

"I don't mean to sound like I'm calling you a liar, but I think you're not telling me the truth."

I turned towards the bar and leaned on my crossed arms, grunting in response with the hope that she got a clue and dropped the subject. No such luck! I could feel her move closer, feeling her warmth as she leaned in to stare at my face. She was going to pry, damn it! "Look, Bud, I'm not going to be a bitch about this," she admitted. "You want to keep mum, that's fine . . . but, as a friend of mine is keen on saying, 'It's best to talk about what's bugging you.'." Her smile was something you could feel; warm and inviting. "So?" she drawled.

At this range it wasn't hard to sense her scent. Kind of like cinnamon, mixed in with expensive leather and a perfume whose name I couldn't place just then... something spicy and heady. Beneath that, I got a whiff of the thick Jamaican rum on her breath and that copper-tang flavor that I always associated with blood smell.

That got my teeth aching again! As drunk as I felt, it wouldn't take much for my baser instinct to boil over. I sighed gustily, trying not to take in any more of her scent. "Look, Maxine-."

"You can call me 'Max'."

"Ah, right . . . look, Max, what I got to worry about, well, it's my own problem." I turned and met her gaze, my every intention focused on telling her that all the cloy, teasing lil' sex-kitten play wasn't going to help her-.

Then, I caught something when I looked at her.

Blame it on the glare from the bar lights, or perhaps I was finally drunk enough to have imagined it, but there was a light of genuine concern glowing in those brown eyes.

Oh, she was still every inch the sex kitten in poise, but it was that look . . . .

"Okay, it's like this," I said. "My life's been a bit... actually, it's gone on a downward spiral, literally! I came out here to see if I could-."

"Pick up your spirits?"

"More or less," I nodded, leaning back with my arms still folded over my chest. "Heard this was *the* place to be . . . thought I'd at least try it out, but so far it's done absolutely nothing for me!" I stared up at the ceiling, squinting into the muted glare of one of the overheads. "Save show me how much drink I can handle in one setting," I added under my breath.

"You mean you've been doing nothing but drink since-?" She stopped, and I felt the small touch of a fingertip alongside my chin. With a pressure that was gentle, yet undeniable, she turned my head back towards herself. "Mister, you can not be serious?"

I just tipped my head towards Joey. "Ask him."

Her head snapped around to look at the bartender - who just shrugged as if he said, *"It's no lie!"* - then swiveled back around to me again. "Bud, you keep this up, and you're going to be sent home in a pickle jar, not a coffin!"

I nearly laughed at that. "Hey, what more can I do?"

"Something better than just flush your life away with the booze," she scolded, even though it was more of a light scolding than a hard case. "I mean, there's more to life that the bottom of a vodka bottle!"

"Well, so far I haven't seen what could make my life better than what it is now!" I frowned at her, as if challenging her to prove me wrong. In all honesty, I never expected her to do much more than talk.

"Joey. Put that on my tab," she said to the bartender, nodding towards her half-empty drink. Sliding down from her seat, she wrapped both hands around my upper arm in a determined grip, tugging upwards. "Come on, we're getting out of here."

For a moment, I didn't resist as she got me

off my chair, dragging me across the barroom floor towards the door. "Hey, what do you think-?"

"That's just it, Bud," she said archly. "You haven't been thinking! How much excitement are you going to find while you're sitting here on your duff?"

I was at a lost for words. "Well-?"

"My point exactly, so come on." Before I knew it, we were at the door and she had her hand on the brass handle.

"Now, wait one damned minute!" I jerked my arm out of her grasp and stood with my back against the door, pushing it shut with my full weight against it. "Don't I have a say in this? After all I am my own person, y'know!"

The moment those words left my lips, I thought I'd said the right thing . . . but, someone in the bar behind me groaned; sounding like they just knew what I was in for now!

Maxine just stared at me for a second or two, only to get this smile that curled around her lips; all slow and sugary-like. She propped herself against the door with one hand and leaned closer. One hand rose up to start walking her fingers across my shoulder, moving in a slow, cloying motion.

"You know," she sighed breathlessly. "You're right! You should have the right to stay here. Stay right here, and be miserable for the rest of your stay in Vegas." Those fingers started tickling up the side of my neck, the fine edge of one nail tracing a line over my exposed ear in a lazy circle. "Otherwise, you might just want to leave yourself in my, very capable hands for the evening."

I tried to keep the lump down in my throat and act cool, so I wouldn't show how much this was affecting me. "Oh, why should I?"

Maxine leaned in, her breath washing over the side of my face and neck as she placed her lips oh-so-damned close to my ear. "I think you just might like it, or . . . are you the type of person that doesn't stand firm to experience new things?"

Yeah, I accepted her challenge. Sue me, Okay!

Whisking me out of Frankie's Bar, she'd dragged me to downtown so fast that, by the time my wits caught up with me, we'd arrived at one of those ritzy clothing and tailor shops that stay open all hours of the night. Convenient, huh?

"I'm good friends with the owner," Maxine explained, after realizing that I wasn't expecting us to be let in. "First thing we need to do, is get you a new suit."

"What's wrong with the one I got?" I'd asked, even as the tailor had started measuring me for a new coat, pants and shirt. I thought I dressed rather well. For a dead guy, anyway!

"Honey, where we're going, you need to look better that someone that walked out of a bad mobster movie!" She clucked her tongue as one of the tailor's assistants brought out some new designer shoes to replace mine. "Otherwise, you're just going to get us both kicked to the curbside."

I tried to grin and bear it - after all, it was *her* dime! - and, in spite of the pricks and prods, mutters and a few colorful words from the shop's owner. It wasn't too long before they were done. The smoke had barely cooled from her credit card as I ducked into a changing room to try the results on.

"Well, shall we see how it looks on you?" Maxine asked, waiting with the tailor and his assistant, as she put her credit card away.

"It feels . . . different," I admitted from behind the closed curtain. "I'm used to cotton and twill, I guess." Emerging from within, I stepped out in my new clothes; a full suit complete with a button-down jacket, slacks and a dark silk shirt and tie.

Maxine chuckled, as the tailor stepped forward to make some final adjustments. "Mm, I'd say the results are good, don't you think so?"

I looked at my reflection in a nearby, full-length mirror. Had to admit, it did look way better than my old duds. The assistant even came forward with a new overcoat — like my old trench coat — and a smart fedora to match.

"Wow," I said, taking the hat and placing it in a familiar angle on my head. "The look . . . pretty damn good, Max."

Turning from thanking her friend, Maxine smiled at me as she stepped up to look at me closely. Giving the front of my jacket a few brushes, she said, "Now, this is much better. you look presentable enough to take out on the town." She reached out and grabbed me by the arm again. "C'mon, Bud!"

I barely had a second to thank the guys and grab both of my coats, before letting her drag me out the door of the shop. "Where to now?" I asked as she hustled me into another waiting cab.

"A little place I know," she grinned. "I think you're going to like it!"

She directed the cabbie to drive to a place just shy of the Vegas strip, and when we got there, I really wasn't convinced she had us in the right place.

"*Hooch's Floor Show* . . . ?" I gave the winking letters of the neon sign over the arched, double doors the hairy eyeball.

Turning back from giving the cabbie a tip, Maxine flashed a smile. "Trust me. This isn't what it looks like."

I shrugged. "Just from the outside alone, it looks like some of the places I used to know back in Chicago." It was the truth. This place had the ambiance of all the dives like I remembered back in the day: bombed out gin joints, smoke houses and gambling dens with old boards and brick facades. Fixtures of weathered plaster and shot-through planes of glass . . . the perfect place for hustlers and street people to gather and try to hold back the night and the day.

Maxine nudged me gently, breaking my reverie. "Come on. I promised to show you a good time. Well, this is the place to do it in!"

Seeing no other choice — the cab had long since departed — I let her lead me inside.

Mind you, I don't know what was coming . . . but, when we got past the doors of the inner foyer, the whole places turned out to be far from anything I was expecting!

Mood-lighting overhead and lamps on the walls lit up the entire place, giving it an atmosphere of class and distinction. There was the feel of elegance with silver and china over fine linen. A long bar of oak curved around the near side, where the murmur of people in evening dress lent to the nice atmosphere, which was added to with a complete, old style orchestra-band and a large dance floor.

I must have looked shocked, because Maxine chuckled as I absently let the hatcheck girl take my new coat and hat. "I'd...say you're impressed, Bud."

"I . . . it's great!" I finally said aloud.

"Good!" With that, Maxine nodded to a waiting hostess, who led us to a cozy table near the band. She barely let me take in the oldie, big-band sounds before asking, "Can you dance?"

I blinked at her off-kilter question. "Can I dance!? Well, yeah!"

Maxine grinned all the more, just as a waiter came rolling up beside us. She sized him up and said, "Bring us some of the strong Columbian flavor here, and keep it hot! We'll be right back!"

With that said, Maxine had me out on the bare square of wooden floor space in front of the band, leading me into one dance after another.

Now, I'm not one to brag, but if you live as long as I have you eventually do learn all of the modern dance steps. What surprised me pleasantly was the fact Maxine seemed to know them, too! That girl never lost a beat or a step, and even that dress-suit she wore didn't stop here from doing some of the more risqué stuff when the band switched from jazz to swing, then back to bluesy tunes and even some up-tempo beats.

As time passed on by, I somehow forgot that I was miserable. Okay, fine! I wasn't miserable at all! I mean, hell, dancing the night away with a woman as drop-dead wonderful — no pun intended! — as the one in my company just then . . . hell, even an old curmudgeon like Old Man Burbank would be smiling.

Between numbers, we took a break for a couple of drinks - by then we'd switched to something like coffee, but a bit sweeter, I never can get the name right! - Then returned to the floor for more.

The most recent song the band had moved into a slow jazz piece; something just made for close dancing. Every other couple that was still standing started drifting together.

Ditto for us, too.

I have to admit, at that point holding this bombshell of a lady in my arms felt pretty good. Her height let her tuck in just under my chin, and I had her left hand in my right, with my other hand on the small of her back. The way a gentleman is supposed to hold a lady when he dances. Never mind the fact we'd both worked up a thin sweat dancing, we seemed to fit together like two complimenting pieces.

Okay, that was a corny-old comparison, but hey whatever works, right?

"Having a good time, Bud?" she asked, her arms wrapped around my body. This close, she could have stood on the tops of my shoes and let me do all the work.

"Honestly?" I quipped.

"No…tell me a lie, why don't you." She had her head resting on my collarbone, and I could feel her smile through the smooth fabric of my shirt.

"Well . . . ." I stalled, knowing she was dying to know if she'd won her little challenge. "Yeah, as much as I don't want to, I'll admit this is much better than what I was doing before."

Maxine just molded herself against my shirtfront, tilting her face up to grin at me. This did two things; one, it let me see those amazing eyes of hers, sparkling like amber-colored diamonds in the warm light of the club. I could've read a lot of emotions in her eyes at that moment . . . but, the second thing I noticed was the pressure of two pebbles of flesh, pressing through her suit top and my shirt, against my chest.

"Max?"

"Hmm?" she sighed, reaching up with one hand to start walking her fingers along my shoulder, tickling the side of my neck again with those nails of hers.

Damn it! I'd half expected something like this; deep in the back of my mind, where all of the best and worst of all my dirty laundry tickets are kept. My reaction to this lady's small advances wasn't totally unexpected . . . it was just the 'other'; my nose filled with her scent, only now touched with light sweat and something more, something that made it all exotix . . . exciting.

Clearing my throat, I asked, "Max, did you have any, ah-?"

"Any, what?" She had that tart flavor back in her voice once more. Pressing closer, she was stretched against me from chest to knees. No way in hell could she miss the one way I was reacting!

"Ah, did you have any . . . plans, after we got out of this place?" Geez, I sounded like the King of Corn!

Surprisingly, she stopped her touches along my neck and looked slightly away from me.

I spooked a bit, thinking I'd pushed the wrong button with her. A weight like lead crunched into my chest. *She only offered to get you out of your depression, dummy!* I growled to myself. ! I felt ashamed for my reaction to her. I mean, she's a perfect stranger, and though perfect she may be for a warm bout of sheet wrestling-.

Stopping in the middle of our dance before starting to pull away, I muttered in an undertone, "Ah, damn!" when she remained looking away from me. "Look, I . . . I didn't mean to-."

Quicker than I could think, her hand came around and pressed one slim fingertip against my lips. "Shh! Everything's okay, really!" She looked up into my face, her teeth tugging at one side of her bottom lip. "I mean, look, I'm not trying to act like I'm some easy woman here-."

I had to chuckle at that comment! "Believe me, from where I'm standing, there's no way I could call you easy, doll."

She gave me a half smile. "What I'm trying to say is that I usually don't come on to perfect strangers out of nowhere." She lifted her shoulders up in a sigh. "I'm no prude either, bud. I tend to be choosy with whom I want to get, well . . . ."

I saved her from trailing off into silence. "Intimate with?" She nodded. "Well, I have to admit, any 'dead' man would be attracted to the idea of becoming 'intimate' with you." I laughed inside at my bad pun. Reaching up, I tilled her head back towards my face with one hand, letting my palm slide along the smooth contour of her cheek. "Lady, I know you just wanted to cheer me up, and you're doing a great job so far."

She turned to smile into my hand, nuzzling it softly before replying, "Thanks, I really do try."

I smiled back. 'You should always be a gentleman.' my father told me. Never mind the fact my entire mouth was throbbing, and her scent was driving me insane, but I still clung to my old man's advice. "I know this might be bad timing but, I'd understand if you just want to call this a night when we leave here."

Maxine stopped dancing and started to pull back, but she only moved her torso so she could look up at me from a better angle. "Bud, sometimes it's best to just let a lady make her own choice."

"Oh?" I asked.

"However," she purred, her mouth turning up into a smile that made a tingle race up from my crotch to the top of my head and back again. "I really, really don't want this to end here. Not now." With that, she melted back into me.

Wrapping my arms around her, I leaned my head down close to hers, touching our foreheads together. Her fiery amber eyes met my own deep indigo peepers, before we let our lips do a little . . . non-verbal talking. That's when I could feel the heat she was generating; like hot pepper that burns pleasantly in the back of your pallet.

"So," I said, coming up for air. "Where exactly do you want this to start, Doll?"

Shaking my head as we paused outside the door of her suite, I muttered, "I can't believe a gal like you would stay, well . . . ?"

Removing the electronic card from the lock, Maxine twisted the brass handle and pushed the door open on silent hinges. "What? Just because of the work I do, doesn't mean I have to stay at the Luxor!" she grinned.

"Yeah, well, I still never would have expected this!"

After leaving the dance hall, Maxine got us a taxi and ordered the driver to head for her hotel. She'd distracted me with a little more finger-walking over my neck — and a few extra kisses to boot! — so I was surprised to see we'd arrived at the Hard Rock Hotel, of all places!

I never gave the main part of the place a second look . . . but now, inside her suite, I began to revise my opinion of the place. The room was very stylish; sleek designs with lush materials. I tossed my coat and hat onto one of the chairs as I passed through the living area to look out the window. A quick glance to the side let me catch sight of the marble fixtures inside the bathroom.

Ushering me inside, she followed behind, taking time to slip the *Do Not Disturb* sign over the outside handle. "Nice, huh?" She asked, pausing at a small end table to drop her purse and room card. Somehow, Maxine had activated the room's sound system, and strains of mellow jazz music began to fill the room.

I pulled back the French doors from in front of the wide window, whistling low when I caught the vista outside; the sight of the mountains, highlighted by the city lights, was something to see.

"Nice view," I commented. I turned around to say more, and the next words failed to come to my lips, as the sight of this red-haired tart — walking across the carpeted floor with a smooth sway to her hips — sort of killed any further verbal response. She'd taken off her shoes, so her stocking feet made a light hissing sound as she sashayed towards me. She had undone the top two buttons on her suit jacket, revealing a tantalizing hint of cleavage before me.

I worked my clenched throat muscles loose,

managing to croak out, "V-very . . . nice."

Maxine chuckled, her eyes leaving trails of smoke as she gazed hotly at me, closing the distance between us. Her nails toyed with the last button, finally releasing it with a soft touch. The front of her jacket parted, showing an expanse of creamy skin, and the middle part of a smoke-gray bra.

"Very, very . . . nice!" I don't think her smile could have gotten any warmer just then, but when she was this close, lord! I could have sworn she'd scorched me!

"Why, thank you," she whispered, reaching out for the buttons of my silk shirt with both hands. Taking a moment to smooth her palms over the contours of my chest, she murmured, "I think I'm glad we didn't get you that three-piece suit tonight." While saying this, she expertly undid the knot in my tie and slipped it off my neck, tossing it to the floor.

Feeling those warm caresses as they traveled from my shoulders down to my waist and back again, I asked "Oh?"

She nodded, "Makes for less that I have to take off of you." Her hands dropped back down to tug the tails of my shirt free, then she began undoing the buttons one by one; starting from the bottom one and going upwards. As more of my own pale skin was revealed, she made little teasing pokes and tickles with those wonderful nails!

By the time she hand undone the top one, it was a simple matter of one two-handed push, and I was bare to the waist before her.

"Oh my!" She paused to stare at the left side of my chest, her eyes flashing green from the room lights as she turned her face to get a better look at my 'battle scars'.

"Hey, it's not as bad as it looks," I assured her, though I knew what she must be thinking of the baker's dozen or so pockmarks — bullet wounds and places where stakes had gotten a touch too close for comfort. Add to that a loose latticework of scars left from knives and other assorted edged instruments . . . well, I must have looked a fright to her eyes.

Maxine didn't shrink back further or turn away. In fact, she reached up to trace the pad of one fingertip lightly around a couple of the pockmarks. "My, my, my . . . it looks like someone walked all over you with stiletto heels, Bud!" She looked up and pouted through a grin. "And me with only my two-inch pumps! Damn!"

I had to chuckle at that remark. "Why, you little-!" The temptation was too great! I wrapped my arms around her and pulled her into me. She must've been expecting something like this to happen, because she met me halfway; wrapping her arms around my neck, rising up on the balls of her feet to bring her lips within striking distance.

My lips touched down on the pliant softness of those wine-colored ones of hers, and mercy, she tasted so . . . good! Just a a hint of copper, mixed in with the heady rum from the drinks she'd consumed earlier, accentuated with her heat. It was like pure candy to a sweet tooth.

Believe me, I know a thing or two about teeth!

Our kiss drew out from there, getting hotter when she parted her lips to introduce her pink tongue to mine. Ever the gentleman, I let her inside, greeting with my own oral muscle before leading her into a deeper French dance. I guess she liked what she was tasting, because it seemed like forever before we broke off, gasping for much needed air.

"Mm," she cooed, running the tip of her tongue over her lips like she didn't want to lose my own flavor. "A nice appetizer." She moved her arms down, dropping them back towards my midsection. "Why don't we get you ready for the next course?" I heard the click of her nails as she went for my buckle.

"Sounds like a plan to me," I replied, even as all my attention was tuned to what those clever hands were doing to the rest of my clothes. In no time, my belt and fly were opened, and I could see the wicked gleam in her eye as she knelt down to deal with my shoes and socks. She got rid of them and then reached up to skim my pants down, motioning me to step out of each leg before she tossed them aside.

"Ah!" she gasped, a smirk curling over her lips as she looked back at me from below.

I guess the evidence of my arousal was quite clear to her from where she was crouched on her heels. "Nice view?" I quipped, crossing my arms over my chest.

Nodding, she replied huskily, "Basic black. It suits you." She rose upward, pausing to nuzzle the front of my boxers before working her way into the circle of my arms again. "Now, you're ready."

I arched one eyebrow at that. "Ready?" I took a moment to glance down at her still-clothed body. "What about you?"

She grinned, reaching up to place a kiss on the tip of my nose. "That's for me to take care of," she replied, sounding smug and sexy at the same time. She gave me a gentle push, which backed me up a step and into the side of the single, queen-sized bed that dominated the bedroom half of the suite.

Reflexively, I sat down on the soft comforter. "Ah, I see."

"Yes, you will." Maxine leaned down to look into my eyes — while giving me a brief glimpse of her cleavage in the process — grinning like the wicked little woman I was just becoming used to. Running her hand down my cheek in a soft caress, she dipped down to grab my shirt from where it lay, before straightening up once more. "You, stay, right, there."

She said that with such heat behind those words, I unconsciously straightened up and said, "Yes, ma'am."

"Good boy! I'll be right back." Turning on one foot, she sauntered off towards the bathroom; pausing at the door to turn back towards me and blow me a kiss, before disappearing within the marble interior.

With a soft groan, I dropped back to lie flat on my back, sinking slightly into the downy comforter. *What did I get myself into?* Considering what this woman...*god*, what a woman! I sat up and started to strip the comforter down before moving the pillows to accommodate its expected occupants. I'd just reached out to adjust the lights, when the tone of the music changed into something that sounded torch-hot and very smoking.

"Ahem!"

My head turned around at that soft yet commanding exhalation of sound. That's when I forgot about the lights. Hell, I might as well have forgotten my entire name!

Maxine was standing there, propped on one elbow as she leaned against the short span of wall that formed the frame around her. She'd lost the jacket and short skirt, opting instead to wear my dark silk shirt like some oversized nightdress. It was wide open, framing the expanse of cream-toned skin from her throat, down past her two lovely breasts with their rosy erect nipples, to her thighs and legs, which were sporting her lace-topped stockings. These were soft gray, just like the high-cut panties that were practically molded to her hips and crotch like a second skin.

My hand dropped back as I gaped at this . . . Geez! I don't think I could have come up with words to better describe her, just then.

Her eyes traveled from my face downward, all the while her lips curved up into a hot smile that melted me. Well, not all of me! "My, my, my! I can see you're enjoying this," she said in that throaty alto of hers.

I nodded slowly, trying not to lose sight of her as she pushed off the wall, reaching up with both arms to stretch like a contented cat. This made my shirt slide over her skin, making a whisper-like hiss as she started to move her hips from side to side; closing her eyes as she swayed to the music filling the air. She then opened those hazel pools and started drifting towards the bed.

Being this close to her, my senses were filled by her entire being; her sound, heat, and scent; a scent which was now mingled with the undeniable hint of arousal. Damn, she wanted this as much as I did!

"Want to know a secret?" she asked, slipping across the bed on her knees. Closing the distance to grip my arms to pull me onto the bed fully.

"What's that?" I murmured, my eyes half-closed from sheer lust.

She leaned in close, so that we were on our knees together; touching skin to skin, chest to thigh in a single line. Her silk stockings and those panties brushed against my lower body, while the two hot, hard points of her nipples branded my chest. "I'm really, going to . . . enjoy this!" With that, she dipped her head to the side, and placed a single, sucking kiss to the side of my neck.

I nearly growled as my 'other' side surged from the sensations of that simple gesture of passion. Believe me, I had enough sexual lust to make me just pounce on her just then.

That's exactly what I did!

"Oo!" she chuckled, clutching me as I bowled her over, taking us onto our sides as I launched a relentless attack of kisses against her lips, face, ears and neck while my hands moved like hungry spiders over her body. Her own hands were moving as well; skittering over my broad back before slipping under my boxers to grip both cheeks of my backside. This time I did growl as her nails scratched at my buttocks, giving me the drive to reach up and delve my tongue into her mouth, probing deep inside.

We jockeyed for position while we continued to kiss and grope. Eventually, I ended up on my back in the middle of the bed, with this auburn-haired vixen draped on top of me. Somewhere along the way, she got rid of my shirt, and was now nearly naked yet looking so damn scrumptious! Straddling my midsection, she was situated high enough for me to cup her breasts in both of my hands. I gently mauled her twin globes, lifting each one to my lips to suck and nibble on each marzipan-hued nubbin.

"Mm! That's-ooo!" she purred, her hips made little twisting motions in reaction to my supping on her flesh.

At that point, I was feeling just as good as she was. Though it was murder for me to keep my hunger -- the 'real' stuff -- under wraps while I vented my lust for her. It wouldn't have taken much for me to start giving in to that baser instinct, but fortunately, Maxine had decided it was time to move ahead with the evenings 'feast', as it were.

"Ah!" she gasped, pulling away from my leeching kisses with her breathing heavy and shuddering. Reigning herself in, she grinned and started to shimmy down my body, all the while planting soft, brief kisses between words.

"Those are . . . some lips you've got there, Bud! Now, it's my turn!" She ended up straddled over my left leg, the fabric over her legs feeling damn good against my skin. She spider-walked her fingers down my chest and belly, reaching the waistband of my boxers. She toyed with the elastic briefly, smiling down at the rampant bulge just under her face. She looked up, her hazel eyes glittering as she ran a swipe of her pink tongue over her upper lip. "Time for the next course," she chuckled; tugging my boxers down with short, playful movements.

"Geez!" I muttered hoarsely, lifting my hips to allow her to drag them down until the column of my penis lurched upward to slap against my skin, leaving a small spray of moisture where the tip impacted on my stomach.

When Maxine finally flicked my shorts over my feet and off the bed, she turned to admire me at a closer range. "Ah," she cooed, brushing her fingertips along the tops of my thighs. "Very nice!" Her pink tongue darted out to lick slowly across her upper, then back along her lower lip as she grinned up at me, spider-walking her hands closer to my groin. Those fingers inched closer through the light nest of hair around my manhood, tracing circles in the growth before moving down to my balls.

I flinched only slightly, feeling the fine edges of her nails as she scratched me ever so gently there. Sensations of pure fire were racing along my legs as she pressed herself closer, moving her hands now along the side of my legs and torso. Her head canted down at my turgid flesh, the hard nubbins of her nipples poking into the sensitive skin along the inside of my thighs.

I hissed through clenched teeth. "This . . . is-

!"

"Torture?" the redhead between my legs quipped, her nostrils flaring as her breath rolled over the skin of my manhood.

I just nodded, fisting the covers in my hands. The sensations forced a drop of my internal pre-cum to form at the tip of my shaft.

"Oh, my! I guess I could end your suffering," she cooed, walking both hands in opposite directions; one up my abdomen towards my chest, and the other towards my groin. "Or, we could go to the next level!"

With that, I had half a breath to suck in before her face dipped downward, and . . . ah, mercy! My entire cock was submerged in a Universe of heat and wetness, and I loved every damn moment of it! I moaned, reaching up to cup Maxine's head in both hands, combing through her auburn locks with my fingers. Now, I'm as experienced as the average Joe when it comes to sex, but this made all the past experiences seem like the first time I fumbled with a girl in an old alleyway; no comparison in style and quality!

Maxine slurped away like nobody's business; often giving me the slightest threat of her teeth, while moving up and down for a few strokes, then going side on side. All the while, one hand continued to gently manipulate my balls, while the other reached for my nipples to tweak and pinch from time to time. As this continued, she started to hum, the sub vocal vibrations taking me from one peak to another.

"Good . . .God!" I raised up on my elbows to better watch this artist in action. Her lips formed a crimson ring around my shaft, which glistened with her moisture and mine. She never went too fast, but maintained just enough pressure to keep me on a fine edge.

Eventually, she pulled off with a slight pop, gazing up at me with a flirtatious glint in her amber pools while she licked our mixed fluids from her lips. Running one hand over my cock, she arched one eyebrow and quipped, "Nummy!"

I shuddered and nodded. "Hope you're enjoying the meal, doll!"

"Not half as much as you will," she said, smiling.

Rising up, she flipped herself onto her back, bringing her legs together in a coquettish pose, showing off her silk stockings. She then hooked her thumbs under the waist of her silken underpants, wiggling in a way that keep my complete interest at large, before sliding those dove-gray panties down and off. Flipping them aside, she rubbed both legs together to make her fabric-covered gams hiss, before extending them out to rub playfully against my groin.

I snarled softly under my breath; animal and very aroused.

"Are you ready for your treat?" she purred,

slowly parting her legs to reveal the center of her womanhood. At first, all that struck me was the color of the fine hairs that covered her junction — gold-kissed red, like the locks on her head — but I eyed the dusky pink folds and lips of her sex. The sheen of hot liquid sparkled there, making it look like it was coated in fine-spun sugar.

I rolled over and turned to face her head on, crawling on my belly to get between her legs. My nose was filled with the scent of her, and it was making me want to just, let, go. Licking my lips, I glanced up at her face; seeing lust mirrored there, just as great as my own.

"Oh! I think someone's hungry," she hissed softly, dropping one hand to caress the side of her pelvis, almost in a gesture of invitation.

I answered by leaning down to place a light trail of kisses along the exposed flesh of her right thigh, following each one with a lick or a nibble.

God, she tasted so good! It was like heavy cream mixed with cinnamon, with the underlying tang of her blood, just under the skin. Making my way higher, I stroked the side of her legs with my hands, following the trail until I was face to face with her holiest of holies. The smell of her sex was like a rich, deep musk. Pure sexual heat!

next week, and we were both enjoying it!

I don't think I've ever met any woman that filled the 'ideal' that most men seem to be looking for in a lover, but from the way Maxine

I leaned back to examine her groove, and chuckled a bit when I saw it. "Nice tattoo," I rumbled.

Her alto voice was thick like syrup when she replied. "You like it, eh? It was just some silly thing I did-Oooh!" She gasped deeply, feeling my tongue tracing the outline of her skin art.

"Mm-mm, it suits you," I murmured, rising slightly to comment further. "And, yes I like it. Roses have always been my favorite."

Maxine chuckled, panting when I moved one hand around to the front of her sex, plying the folds with gentle fingers and easy touches. "Well . . . roses can be pretty, but, ahhh! We also have our . . . our thorns!" Her breathing pitched up a few notches when I found her magic button, and quickly her moans and little mewling sounds laced through them to form an erotic symphony.

Finally, I'd had enough fun teasing her, so I leaned in closer and slipped my hands underneath her body. Cupping one cheek of that delectable derriere in each hand, I hooked my thumbs around to spread the outer lips of her sex. An expanse of hot coral appeared between them, leading down into the depths of her womanhood. The scent now was almost overpowering. I could swear my mouth watered as I pressed my mouth down over her entrance.

The next thing I knew I had a tigress by the soft tail, as Maxine tried to throw herself off the bed while I worked my oral magic on her. Hot wasn't even close to describing how she was while I munched away at her sweet meat!

"Ah, yes! Don't you dare stop, Bud! Mmmph!"

She moaned and hissed through her teeth, her hands reaching down to twine into my hair, the long nails scratching my scalp as she urged me ever onward to complete her rise to the peak. I was lost in an entire Universe of wet, spicy flesh as I alternately tugged at her clit and lips, relishing the whole of her sex.

I felt like it had been a long while, when I felt the muscles in her thigh twitch alongside my ear. Her sex seemed to double it's output of thick sweetness, while her fingers curled into tight claws atop my head. Her breathing and moans were growing longer and longer with every stroke of my tongue against her flesh.

Then, amid a series of rapid breaths, she clamped down on my head with both thighs and let out a high-pitched moan that quickly dissolved into a shriek of release.

I kept up my oral assault for a bit, then slowed it down to let her come back from the other galaxy she was in. The flow of her nectar slowed down, leaving only a few dribbles for me to swipe up before I lifted my face from between her legs.

Geez, I never thought a man could drown in honey, until just then! "Enjoy that?" I asked huskily.

Maxine lifted her face, her eyes somewhat unfocused as she stared down at me. Her body was covered with a fine film of wet, her hair disheveled slightly from her twisting around on the end of my tongue. "G-God," she smiled, shivering as chain of tremors ran down her long body.

I chuckled. "I'll take that as a yes, then."

She lifted one hand to run her fingers through my hair, softly replying, "I'd rather . . . that you'd take . . . me, instead!"

Come to think of it, I did feel my manhood trying to drill a hole through the mattress just then, so who was I to argue with that suggestion? Planting a kiss on her tattoo before raising up on my arms. "I think, that is just the right idea, doll." After a bit of shifting over the fluffy comforter and the few remaining articles of clothing left beside us, we were locked together rather unorthodoxly; with me sitting on the edge of the bed with my feet on the floor, and Maxine mounted while facing towards me.

She had her legs wrapped around my back and her hands clutching at my shoulders. It took some doing, but we quickly found the right combination of movement, pressure and control. In short, I was basically fucking this lady into the next week, and we were both enjoying it!

I don't think I've ever met any woman that filled the 'ideal' that most men seem to be looking for in a lover, but from the way Maxine bounced, twisted, rocked and otherwise posted on my shaft, she ranked very highly in my point of view.

"God, yes!" she sighed.

Her breath was pepper-hot against my face as she rode in the saddle of my lap, her skin slippery-smooth as it glided against my own. Those long nails trailed over my skin, leaving fire-trails that drove me closer to the edge, much sooner than I was expecting!

And I don't mean my climax, brother!

I couldn't stop the reaction then; the sharpening of my senses, taking in each individual scent of her, just like a master wine taster sampling an array of vintages. Her skin excreted that salty, spicy taste of heated flesh, mixed with the underlying pulse of her racing blood. I let my hands roam over her curves, pressing her body closer to mine, bringing that delicate neck within range of my nuzzling lips and face.

Pounding into her sex, feeling every ripple and wave of her muscled sheath, I tried to stave off the beast inside me. I started to mask my intent with slow, torturing kisses across her chest.

"Ooo . . . ah, Bud! Yes, mmm, yes!"

A small part of my mind marveled at a stray thought while I wove my kisses in a zigzag pattern upwards over her breasts and collarbone; no matter how a dame sounded, they always seemed to sound like a stag film star in the throes of passion.

I finally reached the top of her shoulder, and began working my tongue and lips across that surface while I tried to guard against the tips of my canines making their presence known.

I nearly got to where the hollow of her shoulder met her neck, when Maxine let out a gasp and pulled away. "N-no . . . don't!"

I blinked, nearly stopping in mid-thrust. "Wha-?"

Maxine gasped when she started her own return stroke, chuckling at my puzzled tone. "Not *that*, you goober!" Doubling her rocking motions over my lower torso, she groaned, "My neck! I'm not fond of . . . h-hickeys!"

"Hickeys?!" My voice shot up a half-octave in surprise. A dame like her, as complex a personality as her...and she doesn't like to have sucker-marks left on her!?

That, as they say, was the back-breaking straw!

I glared at the redhead in my arms, feeling the power fill in behind my eyes as I let a bit of the beast take the lead. I felt a bit sorry hat I had to resort to this, because up until now I genuinely liked Maxine . . . and to be honest, the rational, human side of me didn't think it would work. She was a tough cookie with a strong will.

However, with the booze she'd drunk and the

fact she was totally keyed into screwing herself on my cock, my lust-empowered mind quickly found its way through to her. Her only reaction to my mental seduction was a slight downshift in her motions and her eyes sort of glazed over in an emerald haze. Oh, I'm certain she wasn't losing an ounce of pleasure from our bedside romp, but now that I was inside her — mentally, that is! — she didn't stand a chance to resist.

I pulled her closer once more, and she didn't object when I nuzzled her face aside to make her expose the long side of her neck, moaning as I licked a long swipe across the side of that lovely expanse of flesh. My long teeth poked out again, and I could feel my lips grow hypersensitive. The beat of her pulse throbbed thick and strong under the thin skin there, and the blood smell was so damn strong! So goddamned mouth watering!

You guessed it: sweet toothache number-five! Only this time, the beast wasn't going to be denied.

I paused, rising slightly to whisper in her ear, "I'm sorry!"

She moaned out a drawn-out response; "Mm-m-m, Bud-d . . . ."

Pulling back, I opened my mouth a little wider, hissing a breath before I dropped her body down three times in succession. I rasped my prick forcefully against her clit to trigger her climax. On the third one, I sank my teeth into her!

"A-AHHH!"

Her blood was everything promised and more! I felt it spurt inside my open mouth like juice from a ripe orange, filling my tongue with the copper-tang and thick viscosity of fine cream. The blood flooded my cheeks, drizzling towards my soft pallet before trickling down my throat . . . . I lifted her up from my cock, still affixed to her above as below, before dropping her one more time to slide my manhood home. At the same time, I gave her neck a brief pulse of suction. There was a quaking tremor that filled her from toes to the top of her head, and her moans climbed in successive pitch with each second passing. I pump-dropped her one last time, timing another draw from her neck.

I didn't want to drain her — god, I'd die literally if I did that! — but, I've found that taking just enough blood at the time of climax often makes the event incredibly stronger. With Maxine, it was no exception!

"OH GOD!" she screamed hoarsely, throwing her arms around my neck, clutching me tighter while her thighs nearly crushed mine as she bucked and rocked against me. Her motions send a vice-grip roll down my shaft, and that tripped my trigger! In moments, we were both howling and crashing against one another in the mother of all orgasms: our flesh rolling with the pleasure that only comes from fine, fine sex!

Eventually, we both hit calmer waters as our trip to the 'summit noble' came to an end.

The air around us reeked of musk and sweat, with a slight touch of blood smell, too. Maxine was still locked around me in a death grip, shivering like she was stranded in the Andes in deep winter. I had the shakes myself, but I had enough sense of mind to lick up the few trickles of blood outside her neck to make sure I didn't spook her if she suddenly noticed.

"Ooh, my, my, MY!" she crooned softly, her limbs loosening their lock on me by slow degrees. Who was I to complain? We weren't going anywhere soon! "Jee-sus, Bud! T-that was . . . w-was-?"

I licked my lips, feeling my canines retract as I got the last vestiges of my little indiscretion under wraps. "Was what, doll?"

Maxine shook her head, going like water as she melted into me. "That, was, incredible!"

I wanted to laugh; telling her it was due to experience. Yeah, about nearly dozens of decades of experience! I saw she was growing more and more sleepy, so I just said, "Yeah, it was incredible."

She moaned, still clasped around me, as she snuggled closer with a small, sexy-yet-cute yawn. "Mm! sleepy . . . wanna stay?" she murmured.

I nuzzled a few strands of her auburn locks

aside from her forehead, placing a light kiss there. "Why not?"

STEPHEN R. SOBOTKA

TWO OF A KIND

2. - Morning After...

Yeah, you I don't know what love...
But I think I must have it bad.
You know some people say
love is just a gamble
But whatever it is,
it's enough to drive old me mad . . . .

— "Gambler's Blues", B. B. King

TWO OF A KIND

Okay, I know you were expecting some
thing more juicy . . . but, the truth is,
I couldn't have stayed the whole night
with her. I really don't think when the sun rose,
that she'd have appreciated finding a stiff man in
her bed.

Not in that way, you perverts!

I did stick around long enough to make sure
she fell into a natural sleep, and that the bite didn't
bleed further. By the time I did make it back to
the third-rate motel I was staying at, I shaved it
pretty damn close! I only had a few minutes to
spare before Ol' Mister Sol peeped over the hori-
zon at Sin City once again.

The following night, after rising from my own

bed — which reminded me how much better Maxine's big one had been — I made my way back to Frankie's to make some discrete inquiries about her whereabouts. Fortunately, Joey's opinion of myself had risen since we last met, so he pointed me in the right direction: she was attending her fashion show at the Luxor itself!

I never expected this little trip out West would land me at one of the most recognizable of all of Vegas' landmark hotels. I mean, for a guy who used to hang out in speak-easies and poker dens, it's a little weird, hm?

By the time I got there, I found out it was the last night of the convention. All of the major events were winding down, but there were a few die-hard people still lingering in some of the salons and the dealer's room. As big as the Luxor is, I was fortunate enough to snag a staffer and get them to direct me to where I needed to go; the far end of the football-field sized display room, where Maxine's booth had been set up.

And there she stood. Geez! Even after cooling off from spending the night together, I felt a new flash of warmth as I took in the sight of her as she stood there talking to two rather dapper looking men in Brooks Brothers Suits. She wore a pair of dark, low-heeled, open-toe pumps, over a pair of back-seamed stockings that went on for miles. Added to this was a skirt and suit coat of rich purple, but cut to look very professional . . .

until you noticed that the hem was short enough to reveal a good expanse of skin.

Her hair was styled in an expertly-set auburn coif, and she had the right touch of make-up on her eyes and lips as well. I guess I shouldn't have been surprised to see the colored, floral scarf around her neck . . . but, even that little reminder of what I'd done didn't take away from my real-izing just what a knockout Maxine was.

I crossed the last few feet between two booths to get within her range of vision. At first, she was too wrapped up in whatever she and the zoot-suits were talking about, so I moved a bit closer, lean-ing against one of the displays next to her booth. Watching while she continued speaking with the big fellow on her right, I couldn't help grinning to myself; seems Maxine could hold her own with the big boy's of fashion, if the serious set of her face and the rapt attention on the guy's face was any indication.

When she turned to talk to the man on her left, she finally caught sight of me.

I half expected a look of surprise, or fear, or something. The only break in her professional mask was a slight widening of her eyes, filled with recognition, before she continued speaking to her two companions. Well, at least she didn't run off screaming like some B-movie queen! That had to count for something in my favor.

Just then, someone jostled me from behind -

some roadie or whatever fashion helpers were called - distracting me while they pushed a wheeled cart full of display parts past. "Sorry!"

"No problem, chum," I said. When I returned my focus to Maxine, she wasn't speaking to her companions anymore . . . because they'd moved off, and she was standing right in front of me!

"Um . . . hi, doll?"

She stared up at me, emotions flickering in her eyes — anger, outright hostility, what I couldn't say just then! — as she stood there. When she did speak, she didn't raise her voice or even whisper threateningly. "Mr. Walker, I'd like you to ome with me, now!" Reaching out, she hooked one finger under the edge of my necktie and pulled me away from her booth.

I didn't even consider saying 'no' as I followed along behind her. We must have looked quite funny to anyone that was around to witness this: this slim redhead leading tall, darkly dressed me along like some prize bull by his nose ring. Wondering what she had in mind, I happened to notice that we were leaving the dealer's room altogether.

Eventually, she found an empty salon, literally shoving me inside before turning to close the doors. I gathered myself...knowing I was in for a reaming or whatnot. "Hey, Maxine-."

CRACK!

Let me tell you something, boys . . . never

underestimate the hitting power of a lady, especially one like Maxine! She's got a punch with more pepper on it than most punks I remember back in the day.

"You . . . you, bastard!"

"I guess I deserved that," I offered, working my jaw from side to side while recovering from the prickly sting in my cheek. "Would it help if I said I was sorry?"

"It might," she said, bristling as she propped her fists on her hips. "But that doesn't let you off the hook, after what you did!"

That threw me a little. "Come again?"

"You didn't listen, did you?" she hissed. "Not that I can say you're not completely blameless — considering were were screwing our brains out — but, that's beside the point!"

Now I was confused. "Huh? Just what exactly did I do to you, lady? I thought you were sore at me for leaving before you woke up this morning!"

"Oh, it wasn't that!" Maxine's eyes were glittering with green fire as she reached up and snagged the side of her scarf with two fingers. "I'm talking about this!"

When she jerked the fabric aside, exposing the side of her neck, the chuckle slipped out of my mouth before I could smother it. I did wrap my hand over my mouth to keep it from becoming a full-blown guffaw.

"This isn't that funny, Bud!"

"No, it is not," I admitted, still smiling as I looked at the results of my handiwork from last night: four, neat pinhead-sized holes, each one circled by a ring of slightly-bruised flesh sat in stark relief against the creamy complexion of her skin. I was privately relieved to see they didn't look too bad. Given a few days, and they'd be healed and just a memory.

"Look, don't you think you're getting a little too worked up about this, doll?"

Letting go of the scarf, Maxine shoved a finger up close to my kisser. "Look, I admit I can be a drama queen — when I want to be — but, out of all the things that really, really annoy me, having passion marks left on my neck ranks pretty high up on my list!"

I just blinked at her, still grinning as I shrugged and asked, "So, lots of people can't stand hickeys. I didn't think-!"

"That's my point! You didn't think, even after I said no," Maxine said.

She was seriously honked up over this! "Look, don't let this get you into a lather, okay? I could have done something worse-!" Cripes! I cut off the rest of what I was about to say, and watched as she backed up a step or two. Shit! 'And the award for the Most Inappropriate Timing in a Morning-After Talk goes to-!'

"Just, what did you mean by that?"

Oh, boy! Well, here's another fine mess you got us into, my mind said to my mouth. Looking away briefly, I replied, "You don't want to ask that, doll. I mean, you really don't. Trust me."

Maxine glared at me. "Unless you spill, buster, we're going to have a talk with some of my friends in the blue suits . . . and I don't mean from the business world, either!"

Ah, hell! There goes the rest of my vacation!

Sighing, I looked at Maxine and said, "Lady, I didn't want this . . . but I guess you're about to find out what a good friend of mine used to say."

Arching one eyebrow, Maxine crossed her arms and asked, "What exactly is that?"

"That sometimes the truth is stranger than pure fiction," I replied, just before I left my mouth open so she could see my teeth . . . and I mean every bit of four specific, pointed teeth!

That angry look on Maxine's face faltered, then vanished as she stared hard at my dental work; her cheeks going pale when I pushed my fangs out then pulled them back in, closing my mouth with a loud click! That made her jump back a little more. "Oh, my god!"

"You get the picture?" I asked, a bit acidly.

Maxine reached up and gingerly cuped her slim hand over the side of her neck. She's a bright kid . . . and, I had to give her brownie points for not fainting dead away, or even screaming bloody murder just then. "You . . . you-?" She shook her head slowly, never taking her eyes off my face.

"Yeah, you just can't fabricate this sort of thing, not without a budget the size of one of Spielberg's paydays." Sighing, I stepped around her and pointed my nose towards the salon doors. "See you around, doll . . . or not, if you're lucky." My mind started mulling over whether or not I had time to get back to my hotel to pack up, or if I should just grab the next taxi to the airport-!

"Hold it, Bud!"

I felt two hands snag my arm, just as I'd closed my fist around the handle of the door. Jerked to a halt, I half-turned, staring as Maxine cinched a tight hold on my arm.

"Just where do you think you're going, mister?"

"Huh?" I blinked. "Um, on the next fast jet out of town . . . I thought?!"

"Not just, yet," Maxine shook her head. "You are going to make up for last night's little indiscretion, starting by accompanying me to a little after-party. Burnaby's secretary gave me two invites by mistake, but . . . I think you can pass for an acceptable date."

You could've picked my jaw up with a shovel, that's how hard it must've hit the floor when what she said sunk into my braincase. "A date?" I sighed, "Maxine, are you losing you're grip on things here? Don't you realize what I am?"

She pulled back a bit, surprised by the heat

in my tone. "You're a vampire. So?"

Now I was completely flabbergasted. "So!? Doll, I'm a walking, talking, card-carrying member of the walking dead!" I let go of the door handle, pointing to myself for emphasis. "I drink blood, you know? Live stuff! Sunscreen won't cure any exposure if I'm caught out in broad daylight, and-!"

Maxine cut off my angry diatribe by gently slapping one hand over my mouth. When I fell silent, she asked, "Are you finished now?" she asked, her twinkling eyes regarding me. "Now, let's you and me be honest here. Yes, I get that you're a vampire, and knowing what you are does shock me. Still, it's out in the open now, so how do we deal with this?"

I couldn't give her an answer, off the cuff.

"Well, I guess I could just let you go, and never see you again?" she offered.

"Do you want me to go?" I had to ask, but the prospect of leaving . . . not something that settled with me just then.

Maxine just shrugged. "I can understand, if you feel you have to, but you could stick around and keep sharing the good times here, with me." She stepped closer to me, smiling up into my surprise-filled face. "After all, it's not like I'm keeping you here against your will and, well . . . I know how tough it would be for you if word got out-?"

"You hit the nail square, doll," I said, nodding slowly.

She looked at me rather solemnly. "Still, I'd hate for you to have to close your trip here, just because of someone you didn't trust?"

Once again, she'd surprised me. "Maxine, you aren't someone I don't — who I can't — trust," I said softly, reaching up to put my hands on her shoulders, holding her at arms-length. "I admit it, there's never been a lot of people around me, with whom I trusted, before . . . ."

"So, does that mean, you'll stay? With me?"

"Are you sure you're completely okay with that idea?" I gazed down at her, trying to read her expression and body language. "We both could be in for a lot of trouble, if we're not careful-?"

That made her chuckle. "Hey, a little trouble is good for you!" She walked her fingers along both of my arms, before she pulled me closer. "Besides, I'm a big girl, Bud. I think I can handle whatever curve-balls come our way." As if to put the exclamation point on that statement, she rose up and kissed me . . . still hot as cinnamon and just as rich as the night before!

Pulling back after a bit, I smiled and said, "Well, I guess I can't argue with you on that score."

She purred. "Good!" Turning us around, she wrapped both of her arms around my left one, sighed and smiled. "So how about that date, Bud?

I can't guarantee much on the atmosphere at Burnaby's, but at least you'll be with me."

I tipped my hat back, making it look like I was mulling it over before I reached out and opened the salon door. "Hmm," I murmured, guiding her out through the doorway. "You think they'll serve Bloody Mary's at this shindig we're going to?"

Maxine laughed, shaking her red-haired head. "Not as strong as Joey makes them, but . . . don't you think you're better off staying sober?" She reached up and started toying with the collar on my shirt. "Considering what may lie ahead?"

I grinned, pulling my arm away before I draped it around her shoulders, pulling her up close as we walked towards the hall's big exit. "Doll, I wouldn't miss anything that involves you — drunk or sober!"

The gig at Burnaby's wasn't as bad as I feared, but it wasn't much to talk about. All these fashion and designer types hob-knobbing about, talking about the newest 'rage' in the clothing markets and what the new lines will be. Fortunately, Maxine was there to guide me through most of it. With her at my side, she kept me from alternating between looking lost to nearly strangling this one cuss that just didn't understand that I was into 'pie' and not 'strudel'!

Of course, calming me down in the lee of a large marble statue in Burnaby's foyer almost led to an interesting explanation when we were nearly caught by this one pair of models . . . like the lady said before, you had to be sober to appreciate what happened!

Later, we snagged a cab down to this little out-of-the-way place I'd discovered during my second day in town; a cozy nook that served hot coffee and cool jazz by a four-piece in the corner. Perfect place to unwind, and catch our breath. Taking a moment to order up a pair of steaming mugs of java, we found a table in the corner and just took in the smoky strains coming from the musicians.

"So," Maxine asked me softly, moving her chair closer so that we could talk without attracting too much attention, "How did you like Burnaby's?"

I shrugged, though I arched my eyebrows before smiling, "It wasn't too bad. Though, it had a lot to do with the company I was keeping."

"Flatterer," she said, waiting a bit as a waitress stepped up to deliver our drinks. "No one will ever fault you for your . . . discriminating tastes. At least where you pick your companions, hm?"

"Now who's the flatterer?"

She fluttered her eyelashes, making a moue with her lips. "Who, me?" Smiling wide, she leaned over to sniff the wisps of aroma coming from her cup. "Mm! Hot and strong!"

I chuckled, reaching for a small silver pitcher of cream . . . real stuff, not the processed junk you get in most places these days. "I always preferred creamy and smooth, myself."

Maxine's amber eyes twinkled, regarding me from over the rim of her mug as she took a slow sip of her Columbian roast.

"So...you always attend junkets like that Glamor-Con?" I asked, stirring up the milky-sweet stuff in my coffee.

"Not as big as Glamor-Con, but they're big enough for me," she admitted, setting her cup down. "Still, considering that the more markets I get the *Bondage Babes* name out to-."

"*Bondage Babes*?!" I had to smirk.

"I have a good friend in New York that's partially into the BDSM scene," Maxine explained, grinning at my surprise. "Figured a name like that just wouldn't go unnoticed out among the other sellers." She wrinkled her nose at me before going on, "A lot of it is just fantasy clothing. Nothing major; body suits, leather apparel, accessories-."

"Paddles, chains and whips...oh my!"

She gave me a soft kick under the table. "Bud!"

I grinned before giving her a mock-hurt look from the kick. "Well, can't say that you don't have a boring line-up, doll."

She rolled her eyes for a bit. "Okay, we might have a couple of 'beginner's' items, but you'd have to look elsewhere for the really hardcore stuff. Oh, we spice it up with some new designs every year." Taking another sip of her coffee, she added, "Maybe I'll show you some of the new stuff I got from the home store just the other week…if you're, at all interested…that is?"

I shot a sideways glance at her, feigning interest in the swing-beat number the band just started up. "Hmmm, well I dunno," I muttered noncommittally. "I mean…I've go so much to do over the next few days-."

"Oh, real-ly," she purred. Just then, I felt something start to slide up the side of my left leg. I didn't need to have the music stop to sense the hiss of fine silk as it moved against the fine fabric of my trousers, or the heat of a small foot against my own flesh.

Ah . . . yeah," I said, trying to maintain my composure. "After all, I have to play some serious card games . . . ah, just found out about . . . a killer game of . . . seven-card stud at th-this one place." The foot moving against me wiggled delightfully higher, slipping up past my kneecap to skirt along the inside of my thigh.

"Hmm, Stud poker, eh?" Maxine chuckled, her eyes glittering in the low light of the café. She'd leaned back in her chair, the front of her suit jacket gaping just enough to show the fine sight of the beginning of her cleavage, while she grinned at my attempts to keep cool. "You know," she murmured, her lips forming a small, ruby 'O', drawing out the sound as she slouched a bit further.

"Kn-know what, doll?" The soft sole of her foot was now inching its way closer to the joining of my legs, all five toes wiggling in a rhythm that started to bring my blood pressure up a touch.

"I think, I just might have a reason for you to . . . change your mind about viewing my etchings," she stated, her voice taking on a little husky tone.

Unconsciously, I crumpled the napkin that the waitress had left with my drink in my fist. "Ah-hah! You t-think so?" Geez! I'd played footsie before, but damn, it never got me boiling like this dame did!

"I don't, think so," Maxine said with sexy conviction, just as her foot curled gently over my crotch. "I *know* so!" To emphasize her point, she rolled the sole of her foot against me, sending a jolt through my manhood that made me jerk up in surprise.

Like a shot, my hand was underneath the table, trapping her foot before it could work any-more magic on me. "You teasing minx," I growled, letting some of the animal side of me seep into my voice. "C'mere!" With that, I shoved the table away, giving me a clear path to her seat. Before she had any idea of what I was going to do, I leaned out while keeping her foot caught under one hand, and caught her about the waist with my free one. Pulling her out of her chair with ease — a fact that make her give of a little shriek of surprise! — I tucked her under one arm and planted her sweet backside square on my lap.

The whole maneuver took less than five seconds, and hardly drew any sort of reaction from the rest of the patrons at the café. Hmph! Must not be the voyeur crowd's night tonight.

"Bud! Maxine hissed, squirming a little in my partial embrace but not really making any attempt to get away.

"Oh, shush!" I said, low and throaty as I angled one hand down to give a small smack on the exposed side of her bottom. "You started the tease! Can't you take it when someone ups the ante?" At that, I cupped my hand over the area I'd just swatted, rubbing it with a slow caress.

Maxine just blinked, before she got this wicked looking grin on her kisser. "Why, John Walker! Are you trying to take advantage of a lady, in a public place!?"

I just flashed her a smile of my own, before making a certain muscle flex under her posterior. "Hm, that would be daring of me," I murmured, leaning in close so we were more or less nose-to-nose. "But, somehow, I don't think the rest of this bunch would be as appreciative of the view as I am." I looked down briefly, taking in the top of her breasts, now pushed up from the nearly wide open front of her jacket. "Besides," I whispered, looking into her amber orbs with a sizzling stare, "I'd rather keep that delicious vista to myself!"

At that, Maxine shook her red-haired head, brushing the tip of her nose against mine before she said, "Bud, Bud, Bud! We have got to do something about your . . . way with words! You could drive an innocent girl mad, y'know?"

"Aw, why curb my natural tendencies, doll?" I mock complained, wrapping her in both arms to settle us into a clinch. "After all, don't they make you well-?"

Maxine leaned in and pressed those soft lips of hers against mine, dragging me oh-so-willingly into a very heated kiss that quickly evolved into one of the French style, lasting for a while before we broke apart for breath. "I think," Maxine said, smiling softly as she curled her own arms around my neck. "That was the whole idea, you fanged goober!"

Needless to say, we could have gone on much farther but, considering this *was* a public place, we both put on the brakes and just let things simmer for a while. By then, it was nearly after one in the morning; the twilight time, where all the nightlife and other assorted sundry gravitated to places like this to wile away the hours before dawn.

So, we drank more coffee, even got up to dance a few times while the band played on. After all, since we both knew what attractions we had for one another, what was the point of rushing things, right?

I'd managed to tip the server a few fins, and she kept us well supplied with brew and privacy. She even got us some sweet confectionary to combat the bitter bean-drink we'd been quaffing all night long. When we weren't dancing, or listening to the music being played while at our cozy corner, Maxine and I just talked together.

She told me about her work in New York; some of her friends and her family, and asked the questions I'd sort of expected her to ask about me: what was it like to live in the early-1900's...what were my first experiences as a vampire like, and *yadda-yadda*, and the whole deal.

I did my best to quantify it all. Believe me, when you try to hide what you are from the world, it's not easy talking about it, even with someone you've suddenly come to trust.

So, it was a bit of a shock at one point, when Maxine tilted her head to gaze at me through her java-buzz to ask, "Can you remember when you realized that you'd, well, become what you are?"

I was dead silent for a bit, then I craned my

own head back to stare at the ceiling, loosing my thoughts in the swirl of an overhead fan. "It was . . . geez, that had to have been the night things changed all over for me." I popped my head back up to stare at her jade-hued eyes, seeing the interest in her gaze. "In more ways than I'd care to remember-."

"If it's something you'd rather not-?" she started to interject.

"It's okay." I waved off her concern. "Actually, it might do some good to tell you." Taking a deep breath, I closed my eyes to collect my thoughts. "As it stands, it might have been the best thing to happen to me, though at the time I was certain it was the worst."

She cupped her chin in one hand, listening. "How so?"

"Because of where I came from," I explained. "I wasn't much more than a street bum; a drifter that lived off the city streets in Chicago." Reaching down, I flipped the fork I'd been using over and around my fingers like a baton, twirling it aimlessly. "I managed to survive by running card games and doing odd jobs. Not glamorous living, but it kept me in some gravy once in a while."

"Sounds like a rough life to me."

I continued, "It wasn't before long when I caught the eye of a certain young lady named Lily Jane Morehouse. She was a daddy's girl and a rebel too! She craved the nightlife, and was always sneaking out to check out some of the dives on the wide side of town." I gave her a rueful smile. "I guess being a rich kid was boring enough for her."

Maxine quirked one eyebrow, grinning, "Oh, I can identify with that!"

"Being eighteen and a young, red-blooded male and all, I couldn't pass up a chance to get with her. Little did I know what I was getting myself into, because she'd kept a little secret from me." I looked at Maxine pointedly.

Her eyes widened a bit. "She was a vampire?"

"Bingo. I never got the full story on who did it to her, though over the years, I have my suspicions." I frowned. "She'd been taking blood from me during our little liaisons from time to time. Over the months, I guess it finally did the trick, but I never learned that until that night came along. And, doll, let me tell you it's not something I'd want anyone else to go through."

"I can't imagine what it must've been like," Maxine said. "But, you were saying?"

"Well, one night we snuck out the back of the club we'd been at all night. Lily and I had been…rather, passionate that night. In fact, we had a short tryst going on in the alleyway behind the club-."

A sly grin slid across Maxine's lips. "Bud…You devil, you!"

I looked off into space with a half smile.

"Anyway, we were going to start up again before heading back in to the club. That's when three thugs showed up, and I mean guys that make your average hoodlum look like a boy scout!" I said, feeling my insides clench from the onset of the memory. "They were looking for an easy score of loot, and with Lily being there. Well, I was more worried for her . . . and I did everything I could to protect Lily — wasn't easy, three against one! — but she kept getting into the fight!

"I mean, here I was trying to keep her from getting hurt, and she looked more worried for my sorry hide!"

Maxine's face fell into a look of concern. "Did they-?"

"Not on your life! I used every dirty trick in the book in that fight . . . think I also invented some new ones, too," I said, before my shoulders shook with a shiver. "It wasn't enough, because the last thing I saw was her getting in front of that gun one of the punks had pulled out." Closing my eyes, I sucked in a deep breath. "I shoved her clear, but-!"

"John, you don't have to continue," she said firmly, yet gently.

I squeezed her hand to let her know I appreciated her concern. "I will tell you this much, doll. Dying that first time had to be the most terrifying thing I'd been through in my life! I can't really describe it.

"Well, when I woke up, I was in the back of an old warehouse. Lily had dragged me there, I guess to keep the cops or our friends from finding me. I can't say which, really. All I remember her telling me was what had happened, and what'd become of me. There was a bunch of other stuff I didn't register at the time, because all I could think about was getting back to tell my friends I was all right.

"But it'd been hours since we'd been attacked, and I'd just gotten back to the club when dawn broke." I swallowed thickly. "At least Brother Stoker got one thing right; sunlight doesn't agree with vampires!"

Maxine nodded, understandingly sympathetic. "It doesn't do us redheads a lot of good, either, sweetie."

I just shot her a wry look. "SPF can't cure the sunburn I'd get."

She shook her head at my bad attempt at humor. "So, what happened afterwards? To your friends . . . Lily?"

I crossed my arms, leaning back to stare at the ceiling again. "Well, turns out the muggers weren't so lucky. Some local beat police heard the shot and cornered them just a few blocks away. Word got out quick as to whom they shot, and the next thing I knew, I was just another statistic in the sad world of Roger's Park. My friends held a decent enough funeral for me, though my 'body' was never recovered." I just shook my head. "Good thing, I guess."

"And Lily?" Maxine prompted again.

"Ah, Lily . . . well, she came looking for me over the few nights after the whole affair," I explained gustily. "She tried to convince me to come back to her home. After all, her parents had to have known about her 'condition', so she promised we could live together."

"But you weren't ready for that?"

"After the experience I'd been though, who could be ready? I bolted. Eventually I ended up in another part of the city, shacked up in some new digs...and got on with my undead life, such as it was."

Maxine added her own soft sigh. "And you never looked back?"

"Nope. It's taken some time but I've managed to get over the loss...Lily was a good kid really. I dunno how we would have turned out if things had been different." Geez, I sounded like some moped-out mooch! Bumming myself out, I'd almost missed the band starting to play a slow and easy number; very mellow, slow and sweet.

"Bud," Maxine whispered, rising up from her seat as she tugged on my hand. "Come on."

"Where are we going?" I asked.

She got me to my feet and took hold of my other hand. "Oh, just about five feet to the right."

Shifting us over onto the hardwood square

next to the band, she pulled my arms around her as she tucked herself neatly against my body. Without further comment, she took the lead and started us moving in time with the music.

I hugged her close, my feet catching up with hers as I realized what she was up to…bless her! "Guess, I needed this."

She nodded, the top of her head just brushing the underside of my chin. "Something like that," she purred, pulling me closer as she sighed softly against my shirtfront.

Rubbing my cheek against her titan locks, I smiled. Guess the lady knew what was best, I figure.

Not long after that, we left the café and were making our way back to the main street to get a cab. Maxine had been silent since we left, though her body language spoke volumes to me; she clung to my arm, her hip buffeting against my left one with each step. I could feel her warmth through her suit, and my nose was overloaded with her scents…

Within a block or two from the main drag, Maxine stepped in front of me, stopping our progress as she tossed both arms around my neck and yanked me down for a kiss; all quick and hot, with lots of tongue.

Startled a bit, I managed to recover enough

to return the kiss, only to have it ended just as fast as it started.

"Bud," she hissed, her eyes glittering greenly in the glow of the streetlight, "c'mere!" She tugged on my arms, stepping backwards and to my right.

I glanced behind her, noting the entrance to a narrow alley looming there. "Wha-...there?"

Maxine could have melted lead with the heat of her stare she gave me. "Do you see me asking anyone else?" Her grip tightened, forcing me to stumble a bit just to keep from falling over on top of her. In a heartbeat, we were in the shadows cast by the tall buildings sandwiching us, moving deeper into the alley away from the lights of the drag.

It wasn't the most ideal of places to steal a kiss, let me tell you! There was your usual pile of trashcans and stacked refuse boxes; the blocky shadow of a dumpster loomed off a short distance away, heralded only by the unmistakable aroma of the city's nightly castoffs and garbage. I'm certain there had to be a couple of felines and rodents skittering around back there.

"Doll, just what are you-!?" My question was cut off as Maxine shoved me back into one of the alley walls. She pressed herself against me, curling her fingers into my hair to bring my lips down onto hers in another scorcher of a kiss! By the time she let me come up for air, I wasn't in the mood to question what was on her mind! I gasped, feeling the fire she was kindling start to spread through me.

She slipped a crimson-nailed finger over my lips, keeping me silent as she started to drift her other hand over the sudden knot in my crotch. With a smoky gaze locked onto my face, she fondled my crotch, urging me onto greater lengths and depths of lust.

"Max . . . I-!"

"Hsssh," she whispered, leaning in to run her pink tongue in a soft line across my lower lip. "Don't speak." With that, she slipped the tab of my belt out from the buckle, loosening my pants with an expert's touch.

As excited as I felt, this maneuver was getting me jumpy! I knew Maxine had teased me in the café about taking advantage of her in public, but hell! I didn't think she'd turn the tables around and take advantage of me! Needless to say, I didn't protest much when she got her fingers inside the fly of my silk boxers, coiling them around my cock like a nest full of amorous snakes.

"Mmm!" She manipulated my sex through the fly of my shorts, her smile taking on a sexy, satisfied tilt as she slipped her hand along its length. Leaning in, she planted a slow, wet smooch on the soft tip before she stood up once more. "Remember what I said before?" she asked throatily.

"Ah, about what?" I panted, not really caring at the moment I had my pants around my ankles and my manhood out in the breeze. All I could focus on right then was this hot-blooded minx standing there; making me want to just ravish her until she couldn't take it any more!

Then it hit me; Maxine was doing to me what Lily did all those years ago! I drew a slightly shocked look across my face, opening my mouth to protest! *This is nuts! What if someone comes along like before, and-!?*

Maxine must've seen the worry on my mug, but she quickly froze my lips with another smothering kiss; this one meant to try to calm me down, considering how long and slow she made it. Have to admit, it did work to some degree. Without speaking, she slowly backed away from me, her heels clicking on the concrete as she neared the far wall of the alleyway, directly underneath the lowest part of a rusted, old fire escape.

Reaching up, she flicked her fingers over the buttons of her suit jacket, letting the two halves part with each successive unfastening, slowly revealing the twin globes of her breasts. With the jacket open, she moved her hands up over her tummy with agonizing slowness. When they reached her hooters, she spread her fingers over the two spheres of flesh; outlining her erect nipples between her fingers as she softly squeezed them.

I heard myself moan in counterpoint to her heavy sigh of passion. Damn! She knew just what buttons to push, all right! All my worry started to melt away, just by my looking at her exposed treasures!

She stared at me from a half-lidded gaze. Blowing me a smiling, pouted kiss, she arched her back as she turned away, keeping me in sight over her shoulder as she stood with her feet spread apart. The lighting from the street, accented by a few stray beams from a light somewhere deeper along the alley, presented her to me in a sort of half-light/half-shadow effect.

I knew what she had in mind next, yet you still could have knocked me silly when she dropped both hands to the hem of her purple skirt, drawing her fingers along the hemline teasingly before she hooked them underneath. With the slow flourish of someone uncovering a piece of priceless art, she drew her skirt up over her backside; first revealing the tops of her seamed stockings; held in place with a panel of lace-accented elastic. Then, the fabric retreated further to show the firm cheeks of her buttocks, twin fields of creamy skin against the darkness of her outfit.

I sucked in a sharp breath, nailed to the spot by the boldness Maxine displayed in front of me. She must have doffed her panties somewhere along the course of the evening, I thought, watching her display her most moist and intimate self before me.

Still looking over her shoulder at me, she bent forward slightly, propping herself against the wall with one arm, while she reached under her belly to cup her sex with her free hand. Long fingers parted the pink folds, now glistening in the dim light as she dragged her digits over her passion center. I could smell her essence; spicy and so thick I could virtually taste it from where I stood.

"Well, Bud, if you've ever wanted . . . to take advantage of me," she panted, her voice heavy with her own need, "Here's your chance!"

With that, she replaced her hand on the wall next to its twin, arching her back further, presenting me with an unobstructed view of her sex. As if to emphasize her invitation, she let out a husky, wanton moan.

With an animal growl, I whipped across the alley in a heartbeat, throwing my arms around Maxine like I was about to make an end-zone tackle! However, I didn't crush her against the wall - that wouldn't have been nice to her breasts! Instead, I hoisted her up against my body, bracing my knees against the wall as I jockeyed her into a more-or-less sitting position on my groin. She let out a soft squeak of surprise, but when she felt my hands wrap around her wrists to guide them over her head, she caught on to what I had in mind. Wriggling delightfully against my lap, she took hold of the iron fire escape above us, using it as leverage as she lifted her ass to allow my cock to line up with her sex.

In no time, I breeched her heavenly gate and slipped inside, feeling her walls tighten luxuriously around my stone-hard shaft. This wasn't going to be a slow one, I could tell that much! Dropping my hands to her chest, I tweaked her nipples as I slowly started to bounce her on my half-lap; making her sex slither up and down my cock with liquid effort.

Maxine groaned in ecstasy, tossing her head back as she pulled herself up with her arms, aiding my efforts to pump her quim. "A-a-ah, yes! Yes! Ooo, don't stop!"

"You wanted it," I husked, mauling her tits with both hands, "You asked for it!" I planted several nibbling kisses along her shoulder through her coat, careful not to get too close to her exposed neck. Moving my hips, I felt her backside smack against my groin, adding to the erotic symphony we were weaving in the early morning air.

"Y-yeah . . . oh, God, yes-s," Maxine hissed, shaking her auburn hair out as she wallowed in the sensations rippling outward from her womanhood. "Give it to me! More! More!"

Realizing this was going to take more effort, I let go of her boobs and clamped both hands on her waist, just above her hips. Grunting, I started to heft her body and lower it forcefully, matching rhythm with my pounding cock. With each thrust,

I could feel the end of her tunnel touching the head; feel the contractions of her innermost muscles as they tried to keep my cock from retreating all the way. Feeling this, Maxine doubled her effort, trying desperately to keep hold of the iron railing as she dropped herself onto my peg.

Together, we were lost in a Universe of sensations and heat! Maxine's moans had risen to cries and soft shrieks, mingling with my own grunts and sighs. We must have sounded like to impassioned ally cats; mating like the wild, feral animals that we'd become, caught in the moment...

"Oh-h, Yesss! I-I'm nearly there," I croaked, feeling the electric spark of my impending release flashing in my balls.

Maxine gasped, "Do it! Please, John, do it!" The fiber of her being seemed drawn into a taught line; her legs pointed out to the toes like a ballerina, her body tense with her own approaching orgasm.

I hit the end of my limits then, unable to contain the firestorm that had been barely kept in check since she started this little tryst. "Oh God, YES! 'MAX!" I slammed her down onto me several times, arching outwards to scrape the underside of my cock against her clitoris; hoping to trigger her tumble into the abyss of pleasure with mine.

"John!" she screamed, and suddenly we were

there! Waves of pure energy crackled down the both of us, forking and merging where our bodies were linked together. I felt her clamp down on my cock in a fierce grip, just as I exploded forth, coating her insides with the essences that can only come from the depths of a man's satisfied sex.

The waves crashed over us for several moments, making us shiver and wobble on a precarious balance, until I had enough wits to straighten up to let Maxine slip off of me and onto her feet. She let go of the fire escape with a shuddering moan, and nearly fell to her knees, so weakened from our mutual climax.

"Hell!" I hissed, realizing that this dark alley was no place for a post-coital revere. Making fast work to stuff myself back into my shorts before dragging my pants back into place, I held onto Maxine long enough to pull her skirt down and get her jacket closed. "C'mon, doll! I have to get you out of here!"

Maxine just gasped, moaning with joy as she buried her head into my chest while I scooped her up into my arms. Clinging to me with what strength she had left, she nuzzled against the fabric of my shirt and murmured, "Ooo, John!"

"You're welcome," I mused, placing a small kiss on her cheek before swinging her around as I stomped out of the alleyway towards the street.

About then, something splattered against my

cheek. A raindrop!? I craned my neck to look up, just as a few more, fat drops hit my face. Swell! Just what we needed, a downpour! Now I knew we couldn't get back to her place before getting soaked. I just hoped I had the strength to get us back to my hotel, since I could tell dawn wasn't that far off…yeah, better to get back to my place. I'd be safe from the sun, and she'd be no worse off than back at her hotel.

Coming out of the alley, more rain began to sprinkle around us; pattering off the brim of my hat and the fabric of her coat. Wheeling around for some sign of shelter at least, I spied a cab approaching from down where the café sat. Lucky us! Pursing my lips, I let out a classic *"Hey, Taxi!"* whistle, piercing the night with its strident sound.

Maxine flinched, moaning, "H-hey! Cut that out!"

"Sorry, had to get us a ride," I apologized, feeling relieved when the cab chirped to a halt just a few yards ahead of us. As the rain started to pick up some intensity, I raced forward along the sidewalk to reach the idling car. I was so focused on not keeping the cabbie waiting I bumped into someone walking towards us, sending them skittering to the side.

"Sorry!" I grunted, shifting Maxine against one shoulder to reach the door handle.

"Watch where you go, idiot!" the stranger snarled.

Ignoring that for the moment, I got the car open and shuttled my exhausted charge inside, then followed suit behind her; sliding in on the worn leather backseat while closing the door behind me. I only got a brief glance at the inside of the cab - most are just like every other one, I guess - before the interior light winked out as the door catch clicked home.

"Where to, Mac?" the driver asked heavily.

"Motel Marco," I gushed, trying to get Maxine settled into some sort of comfort on the seat next to me. "Step on it, okay?"

"Sure, sure!" There was a clump as the old transmission shifted from neutral to drive, just before the cabbie flipped on the meter. "Have you there in no time flat, Mac!"

"Great!" I finally got us situated, with Maxine against my side and myself leaning against the near side of the backseat. Letting out a deep breath, I tried to relax for the moment . . . and that's when it hit me!

From time to time, there's this little sensation I get; right at the back of my neck that just . . . crawls up into my scalp like a line of roaches. It's not pleasant let me tell you, kids, but it only ever happens when there's something dangerous around me! Turning around, I tried to get a sense of what that little crawling sensation was trying to tell me. By then, the rain had started really coming down in buckets, and I couldn't see anything except blurry lights and shadows beyond the back window of the car, much less anyone or anything that could be dangerous.

I couldn't even see where that bozo I'd nearly fallen into had gone to. Funny thing . . . that's where it seemed I could sense trouble from, or so I thought.

"Hey, Mac? You okay back there?"

I turned back to face the front of the cab. My eyes fixed on the driver's, which were staring back at me from the rearview mirror. "Huh?"

"I said 'You okay'? You just looked like someone was tryin' to take a potshot at you!"

Blinking, I just shook my head and tried to smile. "Yeah, it's nothing. Just felt funny for a second, I guess."

The driver just chuckled. "Buddy, if I had me a broad like that, I don't think I'd be feelin' funny!" He nodded towards Maxine, who was snuggled up tight against my side, seemingly content to just drift in her post-orgasmic fog.

I just grinned. "Can't argue with you there, pal." As we moved of into the Vegas night, I shoved the thought out of my mind, focusing instead on what to do when we got to my room.

The following day, I clicked awake just as the sun went down.

Usually, I'm not a morning person — that's

an old joke, see? — since it takes me some time to get moving when night begins to fall. However, this night I sat up and looked around, remembering I was back at my hotel, in my room . . . with a beautiful dame in my bed!

Glancing down beside me, I took in Maxine's sleeping form; all wrapped up in a blanket that bunched up on one side; indicating that it once was spread over the two of us. Maxine must've tugged it off me while we slept. Her head lay cradled on the second pillow on my twin-sized bed, turned towards me, with a peaceful expression on her face.

With a grin, I relaxed and slid back down onto the top sheet beneath me. Propping myself up on one hand, I just lay there watching her sleep. I figured she had to be dreaming some good stuff, since her lips were forming a contented little smile. Reaching out with my free hand, I lightly stroked the side of her cheek with my fingers. Her skin had that warm, fuzzy feeling you only get from sleeping; a rather nice sensation let me tell you.

To be truthful, I was really loath to disturb her sleep. Our little soirée last night must've taken a good deal out of her . . . I know it got the best of me!

Lifting up slightly to look around the room we were in, I have to admit it out loud my choice in hotels is more for saving money's sake than style or comfort. This place isn't a three-star affair, and with the faded paint, out-mod furniture and such . . . well, you can see why I didn't want Maxine to have to experience it first-hand. Not after the night we spent in her room back at the Hard Rock!

Silly though, cause when I turned back to her, I met a pair of deep green eyes staring back at mine. Yawning, she raised one hand to her mouth, before rubbing her head against the cotton pillowcase

"Hi, doll," I offered slowly, giving her time to focus her sleep-muddled mind.

Lifting her head, she fixed me with a bleary stare. "Mm-hi your self," she murmured, frowning a bit as she glanced at the bed, then at me once more. "Um, this might sound silly coming from me, but I don't think this is my bedroom . . . actually, not my bedroom, I think."

Chuckling, I nodded. "Nope. Couldn't get back to your hotel in time . . . so, we ended up here for the night."

"Oh, I see," Maxine said, yawning once more before she pulled her arms free of the blanket, arching her body in a glorious stretch. It was then she discovered she didn't sleep the entire day away in her street clothes, judging by the sudden start and peek under the covers. "Umm, did we-?"

I stopped her quick with a hand on hers.

"Nope, but I couldn't let you sleep in that suit, now could I?" I offered. "Besides, you were perfectly safe with me here. I sleep like a log."

She caught my smile and sighed, "I don't if I should be disappointed or relieved! After all, most men would die to spend a night with me, naked in a bed," she said, one brow arching in a flirting curve.

I laughed, "Doll, I just couldn't do much when you were zonked like that! Didn't want you to miss out on any of the fun, if I had!"

At that, Maxine joined in, laughing with me. "Good thing, too! I'd have been royally ticked if I'd missed any of the action!" Impulsively, she rolled towards me, shoving me back down against the mattress as she threw her arms around my neck. Bringing us more or less nose to nose, she gave me a small kiss and said, "Thanks for being such a good sport last night, Bud!"

"About what? Oh," I said, recalling the events before we got here. "In the alley, right. Look, Maxine, I'm not going to lecture you-!"

"That's good to hear," she beamed, wiggling a bit so she was more or less covering me with her body. Her weight pressed down on me, making me feel her lower body rest squarely on my groin and thighs.

"Ah, well," I started to say, "I guess I shouldn't be too mad. I mean, I know I did enjoy what we did."

"So did I." She punctuated that with a light kiss on my cheek. "But, I feel that you're having some misgivings about the locale?

I sighed. "Somewhat. I mean, the last time I tried something like that, things changed for me. Big time!" I rose up a bit on my elbows to stare at her. "Not that I thought history would repeat, but, I couldn't help but think that something-."

Maxine pulled one hand out to run her fingers along the side of my head, combing through my dark hair in a soothing caress. "Bud, don't let what happened back then ruin your life now. Sure, it was traumatic, but you can't let circumstances you can't control limit how you live." She let her head nestle against my chest, sighing while she continued to stroke my hair. "I mean, someone could come right through that door and shoot us both in cold blood-."

"Max!"

Lifting herself up, she stared frankly at me. "I'm just saying that there's hundreds of possibilities that might happen to you . . . to us! But, that's a lot of stuff that we can't control," she reasoned. "A person will drive themselves crazy just trying to worry about it all!"

Blinking, I started to see where she was going with this. "Yeah, you're right about that!"

Giving me a small smile, she continued, "So, instead of worrying, you should just focus on the stuff you know you *can* control, and just take life as it comes." She ruffled my hair playfully. "That's the secret to getting as much pleasure out of life, and giving some back in return."

I draped one arm around her waist, flopping back down against the bed with a sigh. "Ancient Chinese secret, eh?" I mused.

Wrinkling her nose at me, she popped her fist against my chin softly. "Ancient Maxine secret to better living!" Scooting closer, she pulled my head into the cradle of her arms, surrounding me with their supple strength. "Now, think that can make you see things a bit better, Bud?"

Arching one eyebrow, I peered down along my nose. "Actually," I murmured laughingly, "I can see fine, right where I am." I waggled both brows, looking down at the magnificent display of her cleavage, just under my chin. She looked down, gave off a mock-exasperated sigh, then chuckled just before she swooped down to kiss me on the lips.

"Well," I said when we parted. "You did ask-!"

"Yeah, yeah," she groused in good humor. Giving me one more kiss on the forehead, she pushed up on the bed to rise to a sitting position on my stomach; straddling me with her fantastic legs. "Phew! This is the place you brought me to?" she asked, taking in the room around us.

"Well," I shrugged, dropping my hands to clasp her thighs, "it was either here or the Y, and that still was too far off."

Frowning, Maxine looked down at me. "Can't say that I like the place..."

I pointed one finger at her in mock sternness. "If you start to tell me it needs a 'woman's touch', missy-!"

"Hey!" she pouted. "I was just going to sug-gest-STT-!" with that, she nearly hopped of the bed, doubling over as I took the opportunity to race my fingers up her ribs in a tickle. Her words were momentarily forgotten as she tried to retali-ate; sending us both rolling around the bed in an attempt to tickle each other into submission! Eventually, amid gales of laughing and giggling, we called a cease-fire and fell back onto the bed, arms wordlessly opening to allow the other party to cuddle close.

Breathing heavy, I tried to reign in my laugh-ter, while watching Maxine do the same. We must have looked silly! Both lying on our sides, red-cheeked and panting like two race horses, all tangled up in the blanket.

Maxine got her breath back, long enough to finish saying, "I was going to suggest, that you get out of this dive . . . and come back to my room."

My breath froze in mid-intake, as her words sank into my mind. "Huh? Come back to your place?"

Maxine nodded, rising up to stare at me.

"What? Don't you like that idea?"

"Like…well, yeah, I do!" I stammered. "But, I mean . . . are you sure you want me to stay with you? In your room!?" Again, my father's ingrained teaching was forcing me to be a gentleman, well at the least put on the appearance of one…

"Bud . . . John, listen to me, okay?"

I closed my mouth and nodded.

Patting my cheek, she cooed, "Good…now, I'll be the first to admit up front, I wasn't expecting to be with you for more than one night. Perhaps two, at the most. Remember what I said before, about not wanting to appear 'easy'? Well, I guess it shouldn't be much of a surprise to hear this then."

"What?"

With a sideways glance, she continued, "I could just as well turn very 'easy' for you!" She looked back at me, her eyes wide with emotion. "I mean, these two nights together . . . I can't begin to tell you how much pleasure you've given me, and all I was looking to do was to help you pick up your spirits at first."

I nodded, reaching out to cover her right hand with my left. "I'd be lying if I didn't say you did a great job, doll."

She smiled, sighing. "The thing of it is, I don't want this to end, not just yet." She bit her bottom lip, showing me a bit of insecurity that surprised me! I mean, she was the one who seemed so in control of herself, and her emotions. "What I'm trying to say, Bud, is that I have three more days left here in Vegas. Sort of a little mini-vacation, after the convention. And well, I just-."

I gave her hand a gentle squeeze, cutting her off. "I think you're trying to say that you want spend them, with me?" She nodded, and for the first time in a long while, I couldn't stop the grin that plastered itself across my kisser. "Well, I'd be an idiot to say 'no'. I just want to make sure this is something that you *really* want, Maxine. I don't want you to feel you have to be totally responsible for me. For what you did at first. Understand?"

With a happy grin of her own, Maxine bridged the space between our bodies and wrapped herself around me like clinging ivy. "Oh, trust me, Bud! I really *do* want to spend the rest of my time with you! In any way you want." She drifted off, punctuating her words with a soft kiss to my lips as she let one hand slide in behind my head. Without any further prompting, I cupped the back of her head with my own hand; telling her that this little oral match up wasn't going to finish . . . not for a while, at least!

When we did separate, Maxine sighed and stated, "I want to be with you, John. Back in my hotel!"

I gave her a mock-pout. "Aw, wouldn't it be

great to slum it for a while?" I joked.

She groaned, "Men! I'd rather be doing the dirty deed on a wider bed!" she stated with a bit of laughter. "Besides, I bet my shower is much nicer than the on in this rat trap!"

With a bark of laughter, I hugged her tight and sighed. "Take a room with a king-sized bed and Jacuzzi bath over this slice of paradise?" I quizzed her, making a rolling glance around the dingy room we were in. "Hmm, decisions, decisions!"

Needless to say, I was packed up and out the door before another hour of the night was wasted, with Maxine at my side as we headed back to the main strip...and her luxury room! She had to do a little sweet-talking with the concierge, but soon I had my own key card, and my stuff tucked away in her spacious bedroom.

Of course, we didn't do much more that night, other than cuddle and enjoy each other's company before she had to get some rest - big day at the convention in the morning - so, I was left to watch TV for the rest of the night, only taking a few breaks to check in on her.

Just before dawn came, I moved her over so I could stretch out for my daily session of rest. Before I did let sleep claim me, I couldn't help but look over at her sleeping form - tucked rather sweetly in the sheets, with her head nuzzled in the pillows - and, I asked myself 'just what I was getting myself into here?'.

The answer to that came soon enough, much to my surprise.

TWO OF A KIND

3. - The 'Rock...

Life has a way . . .
of destroying our sense of child's play
But under my wing
you'll be back in the pink;
drunk without a drink

— "Till The Savages Come", Manhattan Transfer

TWO OF A KIND

Now, I said before that I'm pretty good with playing cards . . . well, I have to be. Since before I could drive, I learned to play from the best 'hands in the game. My lessons were taken in smoke-filled speak-easies and backroom parlors, sometimes for the fun of it, but mostly to earn my scratch for room and board, bread and butter every night.

As good as my skills are, out of general principal I don't play low-stakes or major no-limit games . . . the former doesn't provide much take and the later, well, the risk far outweighs the ends, y'know? My game is more of a 'middle-of-the-road' type; where the odds are more or less even all round and people tend to play a little more clean and above the table, rather than underneath it, if you get my meaning?

The following night, while Maxine had to finish up her last few duties at Glamor-Con — she mentioned something about a 'dead-dog' reception! — I decided to take a stab at some of the tables the 'Rock had to offer.

This one table hade a pair of dudes were both playing five card draw poker, and each guy had a pretty hefty stack of chips each . . . clearly, Lady Luck had been in their hip pocket before I got there.

Now, as far as I was concerned, I figured I'd at least warm up a little before I went looking for bigger stakes, so I sat down and offered to put my chips in the next few rounds.

I should've known from the start there was gonna be trouble! In hindsight, I could tell these two clowns were entirely too chummy together. I mean, when casual players get together, and someone has a string of good luck, there's pats on the back, cheers and general well-wishing for continued success. However, these two were hamming it up just a little too much for my taste; calling each other by name, going back and forth like partners at a tennis match . . . that should've sent up a warning flag right there!

Second thing which hit me after we'd played a few hands, was that these boys were clearly cheating. How I could I tell? Benny -- the one guy with a denim jacket -- was dropping some pretty subtile signals to the other fellow. Stuff that looked pretty random. Wasn't much to the random observer, but it was there, and damn effective to boot!

Now, you're heard how Vegas is big on catching cheaters, right? Well, someone up in the glass box — the security room, in other words — must've not been checking these two bozos out that well. I should've alerted the floor manager, but that would've made them ask a whole bunch of questions about how I spotted what their camera's and trained professionals couldn't.

It also would've gotten too close to them finding out just what I am, and while I could trust Maxine, well . . . . I'd rather not have to explain my decades of experience to the local hotel dicks.

Next thing I knew, I was down to my last two-hundred dollars in chips and a short fuse on my temper. "Looks like it's not your night, Pal!" Benny said, before he made a show of stacking some of his chips.

I growled, but kept my features as neutral as possible. "Night's not over yet, chum."

"Play another hand like the last one," his partner, a bald fellow in a garish polo-shirt said, "and it will be!" He lifted his drink and swigged a good mouthful, swallowing as he added, "Damn, you gotta love Vegas, baby!"

"You got that right, Chuck!" Benny said, laughing as he fingered his chip stack.

The dealer — a short, equally bald-headed fellow with a goatee — turned to me and asked, "Shall I get you some more chips, sir?"

Shaking my head, I scooped up my two-hundred and sighed. "Sorry, but I was told once you just have to know when to walk away." I picked up my jacket from where it was draped over the back of a chair beside me, scowling as I flipped a five-buck chip towards the dealer. "Have fun."

"Aw, don't go away mad, my man!" Benny said with a laugh. "Just come back and we'll beat ya, again!"

He was so lucky that I'd eaten a few nighs prior till then. Then again, sucking those two yahoo's dry would have probably made my stomach make a date with a bottle of seltzer-tablets . . . ick. Nothing worse than a sour belly, even for a vampire, believe me!

Walking towards the casino floor exit, I almost missed Maxine as she emerged around the side of a marble column. Not too hard to miss, since she was wearing a dark-colored, suit ensemble over a cream-hued blouse with matching pumps and purse. The skirt also had a daring slit on her left side . . . make for a nice view when she turned towards me, smiling so bright she'd put the signs over the Strip to shame! "Bud!" She stepped over and wrapped her arms around me, leaning up to give me a smooch . . . only to stop short when she saw the frown on my face. "Hey, now . . . what's wrong?"

"Ah, it's nothing," I muttered.

"Not with a sour face like that, it's not." She pulled us out of the flow of foot-traffic, into the lee of the column. "What happened?"

"Oh, some punks are running a grift back at one of the tables," I said, jerking a thumb towards the casino floor.

Maxine frowned. "Didn't the hotel security-?" She cut herself off when she saw the dark look I shot towards the ceiling. "No, I guess not."

I sighed. "Took me for a good chunk of change, and I couldn't raise a fuss about it, without drawing attention to myself, really."

Maxine nodded, before glancing towards the casino floor with a keen expression. "Are they still out there?"

I shuffled us sideways a bit, peering around the near-side of the column to get a good view of the floor. "Yep, they're still there . . . the one dude and the guy in the denim-jacket," I said, pointing the two out. "There at that near table."

Maxine peered long and hard at them, nodding slowly. "I see . . . hm, did they take everything you had?"

I shook my head. "Nope, still have these left." I showed her the handful of chips I'd tucked into my pocket. "Why'd you ask?"

Maxine didn't reply right away, but she palmed the chips out of my hand and made a quick count of their values. Then, she looked around for a second before she asked, "I've got a notion . . . want to help out, lover?"

I blinked. "I'm always game, doll, but-?"

"Good, just give me ten minutes, then find a seat on the floor near those cheaters . . . but not too close." She grinned at the surprise in my eyes, before she patted my cheek. "Oh, but before you do, you might want to ask the security people to keep a close eye on that table when I get there." With that, she turned and started to walk away.

"Maxine!?" I stopped her with a touch on her jacket sleeve. "Just what are you going to do?"

My red-haired lover just winked at me. "Trust me." With that, she moved quickly away, slipping through a press of people as she angled towards a nearby ladies' restroom.

Nearly ten minutes later, I was sitting on a stool near the suspect table, waiting with my eyes flitting between the two rubes — who had continued with their winning streak, as it stood — and the entrance to the casino floor.

Per Maxine's prompting, I did notify one of the pit bosses, and while they didn't like someone poking into their gig, they did go along by watching from another place nearby.

Okay, I admit it . . . I 'pushed' a little to make them see it my way. Hey, a guy's got to look out for his gal, doesn't he? I just hoped whatever she had in mind wasn't too risky. I've seen what some rubes would do, when they were ousted as cheats . . . some of the results came at a personal cost, too!

I was about to get up and go looking for her, when Maxine finally showed up at the top of a short set of stairs at the floor's entrance. I think nearly every head in the place turned to watch her make her way down onto the floor!

I don't know where she got it from, but Maxine was now dressed in a red dress — simple, cut short enough to be decent but still showing ample spans of leg and cleavage — along with some sheer stockings and tiny pumps. She walked with a soft wiggle in her hips that had every male eye fixed on her as she approached . . . and when she walked past, if the view I got of her tush was anything to go by!

Benny and Chuck were both trying to make their jaws work. Must've been a hell of a feat, just to be able to move after seeing her walk up to the table, where she placed her purse on the rail and slid sensually into a seat across from the two jokers.

"Hello," she said silkily. Facing the dealer, Maxine asked, "Is there room for one more player, at this table?"

"Um, well . . . yes, I think we can squeeze you in, Miss," the dealer said. Moving to prepare a new card shoe, he glanced back at her and asked, "Do you need any chips?"

Reaching into her purse, Maxine removed the chips she'd taken from me, making a moue with her red lips as she put them down in front of her. "Will this be enough? I'm afraid it's all I've got on me."

The dealer nodded. "The minimum ante is twenty-five dollars." He glanced at Benny and Chuck. "Are you gentlemen in?"

Benny blinked, then he looked at his partner before he nodded. "I'm game, toots! What about you, Chuck?"

Chuck nodded. "Why not? Hope you don't mind losing, sweetie. Lady Luck's been smiling on this side of the table tonight!"

With that, Maxine smiled and nodded to the dealer as she dropped three chips into the center of the table. "Let's play, sha we . . . boys?"

The dealer nodded. "Ante up, please. The game is Five-Card Draw; no wilds, best hand takes all." He quickly dealt out five cards to all three players.

I shifted a bit, keeping my eyes on Maxine and the two rubes for the most part, but I did glance at the pit boss nearby. He was intently watching the action, as well as keeping another floor employee nearby — big sucker, built like a tank — to hedge any disruptions to come.

Maxine glanced at her cards. Her amber eyes were alight with good humor as she peered at her opponents. "Hmm . . . I don't think Luck's been fair to me so far," she said.

The rubes just grinned. "Well, she's been kind to us, for the moment," Chuck said, beaming at his cards as he flicked the corners of two of the five he held. "What about you, chum?"

Benny chuckled. "Could be better," he muttered, tapping his fingertips on the table. "But, let's take it easy on our new friend here, hm?" He fingered a small stack of chips and then flipped out five into the center of the table. "Just fifty to start."

Chuck nodded, taking only a short stack himself to add to the pot. "I see and just raise you twenty more."

Maxine pursed her lips, looking at her cards briefly. "That's . . . seventy, hm?" She took the required number from her woefully tiny stack and slid them into play. "I think that's called 'calling', right?" she asked the dealer.

He nodded, moving to make the chips into an even stack in the center of the table, before he looked at the two rubes. "Any cards?"

Benny plucked four cards out of his hand and tossed them over. "Give me something to work with, okay?"

Chuck just tucked three into his palm, as he

flipped his last two across the table. "Go easy on him, he's been expecting a big bust all night," he said, turning to give Maxine the eye.

I snarled under my breath, but kept my place. If he tried something, boy I'd give him a big 'bust' all right!

Maxine sighed, before she pulled one card free and slid it cleanly to the dealer. "Just one, please?" she leaned back a bit, sighing as she peered down at her cards.

The dealer quickly made short work of collecting the discards and doling out the requested new ones. "What are your bets now, Sirs? Miss?"

Benny beamed, before he put his cards down and made a steeple with his fingertips. "I'm really, really sorry, honey," he said to Maxine. "Guess you'll be out of luck, for now." He reached down and pushed a good portion of his chips into the center.

Chuck, blinking a bit in surprise, recovered quick enough to put his cards down and shove over an equally-large pile into the pot. "Don't leave me out of this action, chum! I see you, and raise it!"

The dealer looked worried, as he glanced at Maxine. "Miss, the bet now is over . . . ten-thousand!"

Giving him a slight wink, she put on a slightly horrified expression as she faced Benny and Chuck. "Oh, no!" She looked at her remaining chips. "I've only got around one-hundred here!"

Both of the rubes snickered. "Well, looks like you'll have to bow out, darlin'," Chuck said. "'Less you've got some more sauce to put into the pot."

Maxine sighed deeply. "This is all the money I have," she said, before she looked at the dealer with a steady gaze. "I guess I'm out, unless-?"

"Unless what?" Benny asked.

Maxine lifted one hand and crooked a finger at the dealer, rising out of her seat to lean towards him, while keeping her hands and her cards in plain sight. "Tell me, if I had something of value to put up against their bets, could I be allowed to do so?" She smiled all slow and flirty. "Just this once, please?" The view must've been murder on the two jokers; since the low-cut neckline of her red dress was giving them a spectacular view of her breasts. In fact, I could see that they were so riveted by the view, they weren't making their usual silent-communication between them while Maxine talked to the dealer.

Swallowing, the dealer turned to look for the pit-boss — who shrugged and nodded — before he faced Maxine and smiled briefly. "Um, it's a bit odd, but we'll allow it, Just this once, Miss."

Maxine nodded, smiling as she sat back down and, reaching for her purse, she fished around inside for a bit. She stared at both rubes, arching one eyebrow in a clear challenge as she pulled her hand back out and flipped a square-piece of plastic into the pot — her room key!

"Why not just call this for what it is, gentlemen. I'm going . . . all-in." With that, she reached in and pulled out a bright flash of red fabric, tossing it over the chips with a flutter . . . it was a pair of red, lace-trimmed panties! "I'll wager one night in my room, to whomever wins this hand." She leaned over to place her elbows on the rail, holding up her cards in one hand as she flicked the last of her chips in for good measure. "No limits, on whatever happens after the door closes!"

Both Benny and Chuck were speechless, as was I! What in the hell was she doing here? I started to stand up, with every intention to march over and put an end to this little fracas right now-!

"What's wrong, boys?" The pitch in Maxine's voice cut through my rising temper, hitting me like a bucket of ice water in the kisser! She facing the two rubes, a smug smile in place, as her poise seemed set to keep their attention fixed on her. "Did I just put the stakes up, too high?" With a slight turn of her eyes, she flashed me a look from across the table, one that as much as said out loud; *Behave yourself, lover . . . this is my show, now!*

Ah, I got the picture! How could I miss what she'd planned? Playing the sex kitten role, Max was trying to lure these two clowns off of their gameplan and make them expose their cheating alliance before the pit-boss and the dealer! From the way Benny and Chuck were both sweating under the bright casino lights, she was getting to them, too!

The dealer was visibly sweating, too, as he cleared his throat and spoke up. "Well, Gentlemen? The Lady has put . . . all-in. Will you follow suit?"

Both jokers looked as stunned as I had been; this was something clearly outside of their game plan, and it showed in what happened next. Benny, his hands shaking, quickly dropped his cards and shoved the remainder of his chips into the pot. "I'm in! I'm so in!"

Chuck stared hard at his partner. "What!? What are you doing?"

"What does it look like? I'm calling!"

"Against that?!" Chuck looked utterly flabbergasted. "B-but, the chips-?"

"Look man, we came out here to get a big score!" Benny said, giving his partner a wicked grin as he jerked his chin towards Maxine. "I don't know about you, but this pot right here . . . it's bigger than any we've seen tonight! I sure as hell am not going to let it pass me by!"

Chuck was clearly shaken. "You're not serious?! Dude-!"

"Look, if you don't wanna, just fold then," Benny hissed. "I'm not gonna cry for you, if you miss out on the chance of a lifetime!" Before long, the two jokers had abandoned all semblance of being casual players as they started to mutter to one another.

Yep, Maxine's plan got to them, all right! I wrapped my arms around my chest, barely able to keep silent for all that I was laughing inside, and waited to see what happened next.

"Sir, I have to ask," the dealer interrupted Benny and Chuck's verbal back-and-forth. "Are you all-in?" He looked pointedly at Chuck. "You cannot continue unless you can raise or call."

When they finally turned back to the table, Chuck scowled while Benny looked smug and triumphant. With a snort, the shorter fellow shoved his remaining chips in. "Fine, I'm in!"

Maxine smiled. "I do like a man who's not afraid to take risks."

"Best get ready then, darlin', cause this is one risk you might not want to have taken," Benny said archly.

The dealer sighed and motioned towards all three players. "Cards please, gentlemen . . . and Miss," he said. "Best hand will win."

Chuck flipped his cards over, scowling darkly as he showed a pair of nines. "I got a pair," he muttered. "Happy now?"

Benny grinned — a look I particularly didn't care for! — then, he looked at Maxine as he turned his cards over. "A pair of Kings, darlin'! Looks

like Luck continues to be my Lady tonight!" As
he started to reach for the center of the pile with
his large paw, he chuckled. "This is gonna-!?"

Just a scant fingertip's length from reaching
Max's pantines, Benny's hand was stopped by one
of her own when it slapped down in front of it.

"Huh!?" He looked back up into her face.

"I'm so sorry to have to burst your bubble,
Benny," Maxine said as she brought her other
hand around, fanning her five cards out as she
held them for all to see. "I'm afraid you two
gentlemen are no match for the House. Especially
this one, boys!"

I rose up to peer over everyone, and nearly
barked with laughter! Damn, if she didn't have
the luck, because she had a full house!

"What in the hell-?" Benny looked down at
her cards, his face turning pale, then red as his
blood started to boil. "Why you-!"

"I wouldn't go flying off the handle, just
now," Maxine purred, nudging his hand away as
she propped herself up on the edge of the table.
"Considering, that there's some gentlemen behind
you that would like to have . . . a few words with
you two jokers."

"Huh? What are you-?" Chuck asked, as he
and Benny turned around slowly, their eyes going wide at the sight of the six, huge, smartly-
dressed men flanking the pit-boss.

"Gentlemen, if you'll just come off the floor

with us?" the pit-boss said firmly, before they could turn and bolt. "There's some video tape we'd like to go over with you!"

The point wasn't lost on Benny and Chuck, who just let their shoulders sag as they let the goons surround them and start leading them off the floor.

As she retrieved her room key and the panties, Maxine said loud and clearly to the two rubes, "Looks like you two jokers couldn't beat this fabulous 'pair'!" She shook her upper body, making the exposed tops of her breasts shimmy in the confines of her dress. "Oh, but don't go away mad. Just go and . . . don't come back."

The dealer was chuckling as he shook his head, watching the whole scene unfold before him. "Sweet mercy, ma'am," he said. "I've never seen something like that go down before!"

"Probably won't ever again," Maxine said brightly, shooting a look my way. "If I know someone, like I know someone," she added cryptically.

As such, I just sat where I was, waiting until Maxine had finished some business of some sort with the dealer, before she stepped away from the table and started walking towards the exit. She didn't get too far along the floor before I stood up and joined her. "I can't believe it!" I said, coming up alongside her as we mounted the steps. "I just can't believe what you just did-?"

"That, is why you are going to treat me to a luxurious dinner, back in our room tonight, Bud." Maxine smiled, as she handed me a card — one of those that the hotel guests used to keep track of the 'comps' they earn.

"What's up with this?"

"The dealer got word from his boss, we're entitled to a quarter of what those goons had filched all night long. The rest will be given back to what other guests, after the crew tracks them down on the security tapes."

I flipped the card over, blinking. "How much is on here?"

"Oh, roughly seven-thousand dollars, according to the dealer," Maxine said, arching one eyebrow as the amount made me come to a sudden stop at the casino entrance.

"Seven-Gees?" I mumbled.

"Think that will be enough? I mean, if you ask me, I was thinking it's just enough for a fine lobster and some good, rare steak? Perhaps some of that good wine I saw earlier-."

Laughing, I looked at her and shook my head. "Geez, doll! That's probably more scratch than I see on one of my bad nights!" Regarding her, I realized I'd have to watch my step around this dish of a redhead. "Remind me never, ever get on your bad side, Maxine!"

Maxine laughed, reaching up to curl one arm around me as she stroked the side of my face with the other. "Just be glad I do like you, you big goober," she purred. "Now, about that dinner-?"

"Hold it! Before we go anywhere, doll," I said. "I just gotta know one thing." I looked down at her hand, where she still had those red panties clutched in her fingers, along with her room key. "Do you always keep a spare set with you, or did you play that entire hand 'commando'?"

With a smoky look, Maxine just curled her fingers around my tie and tugged me towards the hotel foyer. "Well, there's just one way you're going to find out now, isn't there, Bud?"

Growling, I followed her out towards the elevator, and . . . damn, if my teeth didn't start aching, again!

Back in her room, some time after dinner, Maxine called out from the bedroom. "John? Can you swim?

"Huh?" Looking up from where I was flipping through some playing cards — playing a solo round of solitaire — while sitting on the plush couch in the living room-part of the suite, I shifted to stare at the open doorway of her bedroom. We'd finished our complimentary dinner a short while ago, and now it was sometime after ten o'clock.

"I said," Maxine's voice echoed from behind the bedroom walls, "can vampires swim?"

Puzzled, I asked, "Why so curious, doll?"

"Well," she drawled, "I managed to wrangle the night manager to letting me have access to the pool area tonight."

"Oh, is that right?" Looking back at the cards, I dropped a five of hearts over the four of clubs, my eyebrows quirking upward a bit. "Thinking of taking a dip?"

"Uh-huh." There came the sound of her bare feet, padding on the soft carpet as she approached the open doorway. "So, I was wondering . . . ?"

When I looked up, after she trailed off into silence, I sucked my breath in between my teeth when she filled my vision. "Sweet, mercy!" The cards in my fingers slipped out from between them, falling forgotten to the floor as I walked my eyes up and down her body; wrapped in a bathing suit that would have been scandalous from where I'd originally come from. Hell, it looked one-hundred percent more erotic than if she'd been standing there stark-naked! It was a flattering little number — what did they call it again? A maillot? — with a blue-on-gray cheetah-print pattern that went from the plunging neckline all the way to the high-cut legs, accented with some spider-web like side panels that revealed a delicious view of her body underneath.

"I was just wondering," Maxine said, in that slow, sweet way I'd come to know so well. "If there was a chance that you'd be . . . interested in joining me? After all, they do say one should never 'swim' without a buddy." She cocked her hip, leaning on the door frame while planting one slim hand at her waist in a classic, sexy pose. "Would you be my 'buddy', Bud?"

I got my voice back after a moment, coughing slightly to clear my throat of the sudden huskiness. "W-well, I think it would be great!" I frowned, "I don't have any trunks, though."

Chuckling, Maxine nodded towards the bedroom. "I figured you didn't. So, while you were getting your stuff from La Roach Motel, I did a little shopping."

"Lady…we're gonna have to talk about your rampant acts of generosity."

Maxine just grinned and gave me a ticklish poke in my ribs. "You can thank me now, and spank me later. Now, go see what I got for you and let's get going. We only have the deck for a couple of hours!"

"Sounds good, to me." I rose from the couch, shaking my head though I smiled as I walked towards her, aiming a playful swat at her backside, which earned a squeak of a yelp when my palm cracked against her skin.

"Bud!"

"Oh, hush! I won't be that long-." My voice trailed off as I stepped into her room, casting my eyes around to see what she had laid out for our little venture. Aside from the slightly rumpled bed, and a few of the drawers of the obligatory dresser laid open, I almost missed the dark-colored shopping bag on the bedside chair. Stepping over, I pulled the opening apart by the jute-cord handles . . . and jerked by head back up in surprise! Peeking back down again, it took me several eye-blinks to realize I wasn't just hallucinating! "Max!?"

"Isn't it the most adorable suit?" She poked her head around the doorjamb, eyes twinkling with barely-held back mirth. "Don't be bashful, Bud!"

I could feel the smile in her words. Damn! She had a really twisted sense of humor, all right! I reached in and pulled out the scrap of fabric she called a 'suit'; barely a pair of triangles held together with a shoestring, from what I saw. "Doll, be serious!"

At that, Maxine let out a rich laugh before saying, "Oh, Bud! You should see yourself! "Can't I have a little joke at your expense, once in a while?" She came over and plucked the suit from my hand, twirling it as she made a mock pout at me. "Come on now. Do you really think you'd be comfortable in a suit like this?"

I gave her a scowl, but it melted away before her good nature. "Well, you have to admit, this one was pushing things a little, doll."

She stuffed the tiny suit back into the bag, before turning to pull out another bag — less fancy looking, but still speaking of Vegas style — and handed it to me. "I got these for you to wear, for real now." She took a moment to pull out a pair of classic-style swimming pants, holding them up to me. "Will these do?"

"I guess these will do," I said, taking them from her, leaning over to give her a quick peck on the cheek. "So, I guess you could be forgiven for your little joke."

With a smile, Maxine patted me on the cheek and said, "We're wasting time then. The pool deck awaits us . . . my Buddy!"

Rolling my eyes heavenward, I let go of the bag and started to shrug out of my lounger top. "I'm sure glad you're enjoying your little fun, doll."

"Oh, believe me," Maxine purred, watching me undress, "before this night is over, you're going to find out just how much, I'm, enjoying, this."

Not too much later, Maxine and I stepped out of the elevator and made our way across the lobby, following the signs towards the pool deck. We didn't run into any problems — nosy staff or any other patrons with the same idea as we did — as we exited the foyer. About the only person we did run into was the guy at the concierge night-desk . . . and all he did was smile and go back to reading something I couldn't see.

The short trip down the foyer brought the

scent of chlorinated water to my nose, mixed in with the scents of the nighttime air outside. Well, at least this was an open-air affair! I thought, looking out over the vista of the pool deck. Don't care much for enclosed pools, since they sometimes had the feel of a tomb; with all the marble and tile walls and such . . . ick!

Stepping through the glass doors that were unlocked — as she'd arranged for us — I watched as Maxine rummaged for the standing door locks, snapping them home before she pulled something out from behind a nearby cleaning cart. "What's that?"

She crooked her eyebrows at me, grinning as she showed me the "*POOL CLOSED*" placard. "Got to keep out any unexpected arrivals," she explained. Hanging it on the door, she turned around and threaded her arm through mine. "Shall we?"

"At this point, how can I say no?" I sighed, allowing her to pull me along as she headed out into the open deck.

Since it was night, most of the chairs and tables were stacked up and pushed to the side. Maxine had managed to get a couple of them moved over to pool side, where she set us up for our moonlight dip.

"Mmmm," she stretched her arms overhead, taking a moment to slip out of her sandals before turning to me. "Feel that night air! Looks like a great for a swim, don't you think?" With that, she undid the belt of her robe and smiled at my lingering hesitance to disrobe. "Well, Bud? Aren't you going to take that off?"

"Kinda eager, aren't you?" I asked archly. "Didn't you get enough of a show when I put these on?" With that, I pulled my robe open, revealing the dark, classically-styled swim trunks she'd bought.

"Aww, can't I have my cake and eat it, too?"

I saw the laughter behind her little-girl act. "Be careful what you ask for, Max." I gave her a smile, with a hint of my long-teeth showing.

"Ooo! That a promise?"

Laughing, I shucked my robe and planted my hands on my hips. "Doll," I drawled. I should have known better than to complain.

Maxine stepped close to me, running on fingertip along one side of my chest playfully. "Aw, come on... still sore over that Speedo? I think you would have looked very, very nice in it," she purred.

"I'd have been practically naked," I muttered, losing some of my frown as she did this.

"Trust me, I saw some other suits that leave nothing to the imagination." She reached up and put her arms around my neck, smiling with a little more softness in her teasing. "C'mon, now! I think you really do like the way I look, at least. Right?"

Heaving a dramatic sigh, I cracked a smile

while staring down at her. "Nah. How could I stay mad at you? Would ruin the whole evening if I did."

With a laugh, Maxine gave me a quick kiss. "Now, you're getting the idea." She slipped out of my arms and nodded towards the pool. "Shall we get wet?" she smiled.

Okay, sue me if I sound like I went a little goofy, but it was just the way she looked at me just then all smiles with a hint of a challenge in her amber eyes. Grinning, I moved quicker than she was prepared for, stepping forward to scoop her up into my arms. She gasped in surprise, barely able to get a single word out before I turned around once and tossed her towards the water, launching her in a sudden flurry of arms and legs. She managed a high-pitched shriek before she hit the water, sinking down before surging back up to the surface, shaking her head and coughing.

"How's the water, Max?"

When she got her breath back, Maxine shot me a dirty look. "You . . . you did that on purpose!"

I just laughed. "Yeah, I did. What's wrong?"

Wiping her eyes clear, Maxine just snorted. "Nothing, I just prefer to dive on my own terms!"

"Does that also include splashing?" I asked.

"What?" Maxine barely got the question out, just before watching me leap out into the water, tucking my legs up to perform a perfect, ten-point cannonball. The look on her face was priceless. Well, what I caught before I sank to the bottom of the pool, laughing to myself. I didn't stay down long, coming back up to the side, just in time to catch a face full of chlorinated water myself.

"Hah-hah! Very funny, you!" Maxine had her hands pulled back, ready to send another wave splashing against me, her eyes flashing with emotion.

I shook the water out of my face and grinned, "Hey, now who's getting mad?" That caught her off-guard for a bit, giving me time to face her. "Come on, doll... you wanted to get me down here to join you in this little outdoor tub! Well, you've succeeded... so?"

At that, Maxine stopped getting upset and let her arms drift back under the water. "Oh, you!" she said with a smile, moving towards me like some vision out of a swimsuit dream. When she got close, she latched onto me like a barnacle; arms and legs around me tight as she let a smile curl around her lips again. "I just didn't expect you to hit me with some old-school, kid's prank like that."

With a laugh, I wrapped one arm around her waist and replied, "What can I say, Max? You just bring out the best in me."

Laughing with me, she countered, "Isn't that the 'worst'?"

"Depends on your point of view," I shrugged.

"Besides, didn't we come down here to have fun?"

So, with that, we started in having some good, clean water fun, right there in the middle of the Las Vegas night. Now, before you think of that old yarn about vampires and moving water, let's get it straight; a pool doesn't count. It's just enclosed in a concrete hub, and doesn't flow in or out of anything. So, by most accounts, I wasn't breaking any rule by swimming in it. Truth be told, since I wasn't limited by breathing as much as I needed to, I could stay under longer than Maxine could. This had advantages as we fooled around, playing dunking and all the other silly games you usually do when swimming. Of course this also had an extra perk for me, since I could stay under and watch her slim form cut through the water from below, while she swam a few laps to stretch out her muscles.

Brother, what a view it was, too!

Eventually, Maxine — even as fit as she was — go tired enough to just climb out and rest on the lounge chairs near the edge of the pool. "What's wrong? Giving up on me?" I asked.

"Hey, even I have my limits," Maxine said, wrinkling her nose at me as she dried her arms and legs. "Besides, I feel the need to soak up some rays."

I looked up into the night sky, then back at her with a puzzled expression. "Rays? Doll, that's not the sun up there!"

"So?" She chuckled, pulling out a bottle of lotion from the pocket of her discarded robe. "Is there a law that says a girl can't have a *moon*-tan if she wants? When you have a complexion like mine . . . doesn't pay to end up looking like a tomato," she quipped, before she slipped a pair of sunglasses on and leaned back in her lounger to relax.

She had me there. "Suit yourself," I shrugged, shoving off the side to begin swimming a few laps across the pool. Maxine was certainly not your average dame, I thought privately.

I must've went on autopilot for a while — just alternating strokes as I pulled along the length of the pool — because when I finally decided to stop and check on Maxine, she wasn't in the lounger.

For that matter, she wasn't anywhere in sight on the pool deck!

I got over to the side and hoisted myself onto the concrete edge and took a quick stock: her towel and robe were still next to the chair, as were mine... the doorway leading out looked undisturbed as well, and there didn't appear to be any signs of foul play that I could see.

That was some comfort . . . only just.

"Maxine?" No reply. Was she hiding? I looked around the deck with a more measured gaze, but with all the chairs packed up, tables pushed to, and the few cabanas locked tight, there seemed little place that a grown woman like Maxine could hide in. "Max!?" Nothing.

Okay, so I was a little worried, but after all, we were in the hotel still. What could possibly happen to a big girl like her?

Nonetheless, I got out of the pool and started moving around, peering into every corner, nook and shadow that I hadn't been able to view from the waterside. Stepping up on the ledge of the waterfall, sitting on the pool's far side. Pretty nifty piece of work. I mean, sure you don't find natural waterfalls in the middle of Nevada, but from the way the builders worked it, you'd swear they ripped it right out of some tropical jungle and dropped it there.

Moving carefully, I got to the space just beside the waterfall itself; clear water rushing over the lip of an overhanging rock, over the ledge into the pool. From there, I had a better view of the entire pool area, but there was still no sign of her! "Okay, Doll! Where are you?" I called out. "C'mon, this is getting old, and I ain't getting any younger!"

Just then, someone chuckled . . . right behind me!? Turning around, I peered through the sheet of moving water, where I caught sight of one of Maxine's legs; curling around the corner of a small cave-like entrance behind the sheer wall of water.

"Max?!"

"Uh-hmm?" An arm and that auburn-haired head joined the distorted image, moving closer to the water in a slow, feline-like glide. The water parted like a curtain on opening night, as her hand and forearm emerged, one finger crooked in an inviting gesture.

"Doll," I said, trying not to sound too upset as I grinned inwardly at her theatrics.

"What's wrong, Bud?" She started to move her hand in a sinuous, weaving motion, almost as if it was a cobra, dancing to the tune of a snake charmer. "You're not afraid of getting . . . wet, are you?"

"A little water never bothered me before," I said, stepping closer to the moving wall of water. Before I could do or say anything further, her hand shot out, snagged the waistband of my trunks and boldly jerked me forwards.

"Hey!" Unable to do much more than let my body follow, I sputtered as I crossed through the cascading water; off-balance, tumbling until I felt a pair of arms wrap around me and — twisting with our forward momentum — I landed on my backside in the dim light of the grotto behind the falls!

With a very-pleased and smug looking red-head on top of me! "Surprise!"

"Very funny, doll," I grumbled, grimacing

from the sudden stop as I took a quick glance around us; seeing a small, natural-looking cul-de-sac of a chamber, with what looked like another dark curtain of water, rushing on behind us. Hell of a mood-setting, I had to admit, even with a sore butt. "Ow!"

"Aw, did you hurt yourself, Buddy?" Maxine asked playfully. "I could kiss it, and make it all better?"

I shook my head. "Nah, it's alright," I said, looking up at her as she lay over me. "So, what's the game, now that you've obviously got me where you want me?"

Maxine chuckled, her rich voice echoing off the grotto walls. "Oh, just a private, kinky little game between you and me. Interested?"

I had to laugh at her sly expression. "I'm always up for a friendly game, Doll."

"Good. C'mere!" She leaned down, and engaged her lips and mine in a kiss that could've literally filled the air with steam. "Hmmm!" Pulling back at the end of it, her green eyes glowing as she stared back at me. "Tasty," she murmured, licking her lips.

"You're pretty scrumptious yourself!" I gasped.

Running one hand over my chest, Maxine chuckled briefly before she purred, "Well, as delicious as your kisses are, Bud, I'm hungry for something a little more . . . substantial!"

"Oh, really?" I got an inkling of where this was headed to, when she rose up and pulled her knees alongside my waist; straddling my midsection as she continued to caress my chest and shoulders with soft, slow motions.

With a smoky gaze, Maxine sighed and pulled her hands down my torso, circling my navel before she raised them up and dragged them sinuously over her own body. With a feline hum that was full of the promise of passion, she let her fingers trail up towards the upper part of her swimsuit, toying briefly with the straps over her shoulders before she slipped them down and off, letting the blue-leopard print material bunch around her upper arms. There was a pause, then she worked her arms free of the suit top and let it fall down the rest of the way . . . .

Lord, you had to be there, just to be able to appreciate the situation! Sure, I was lying flat on a rough, rocky surface, with the smell of chlorinated water all around. Not to mention being slightly cool from all the soaking I'd gotten. Yet, to look up and see this living doll of a dame — topless, with her nipples firming up from the cool air and her own internal heat — sitting on my crotch, which was generating a heavy heat of its own . . . well, I wouldn't want to be anywhere else, let me tell you!

"Holy, heaven . . . Max!" I hissed a breath through my teeth, lifting my hips up a bit to let her know just what effect she was having on me.

With a smile, she closed her eyes and slowly rolled her hips; making that delicious peach of a bottom grind against me. "Mmm, now . . . I'm feeling something that I know I'm going to, just, relish!" With that, she dropped back down until both of our fronts were touching — her nipples like cherry stones against my skin! — as she ghosted several teasing kisses across my lips.

All I could do was moan, lifting my hands to clutch at her arms . . . only to find her gripping my wrists and forcing them down against the rocky surface beneath me.

"Uh-uh, Bud," she said, her voice heavy and thick. "Are you gonna let me have my treat, or do I have to get rough with you?"

I nodded. "I'll be good, doll."

With a grin, she leaned up and left a light peck on the tip of my nose. "Good boy. Now . . . stay put!"

With that, she let go of my wrists and slowly started to slither back along my body, all while trailing more lip prints that seared into every inch of skin she came in contact with. Following with fingers that lingered to caress, she made progress over my chest, down each side to tickle my ribs, then over my stomach. Stopping there to tease briefly, she was soon at eye-level with my waist while she crouched over my legs. With a deft poke under the waistband of my bathers, she gripped the loose end of the ties holding them up and tugged, all while her eyes were aflame as she looked up at me.

Unblinking, I stared back and flared my nose to drink in the new presence of her aroused scent. "Ooh, man!"

With a panting chuckle, Maxine pulled the tie and quickly got it undone, letting it go before she tucked three fingers on each side of my hips, pulling down on my trunks with steady force. Unable to resist, I lifted up and she got them down to the middle of my thighs . . . and if there was any doubt as to my arousal before now, Maxine got a good view of things as my hard dick popped free of its confinement.

"Ahh," she sighed, smiling as she got an eye-ful of the hard column of flesh before her. "That's the tender morsel I've been craving . . . all night long!" Reaching up, she curled the fingers and palm of her left hand around my cock and cradled it gently. The warmth of her hand around my hot-ter flesh was a contrast that sent my libido soaring.

"Ah-ahh . . . umm, man!" I did my best to keep myself quiet — Lord knows how the echo inside this place could've been heard, if it got to anyone outside on the pool deck! Trouble was, when Maxine started sliding her hand up and down, one steady pull after another . . . well, volume was the least of my worries just then!

Inching closer, my redheaded lover parted her lips to let her breath coat the taut skin of my cock head; the sensations making sparks race up my entire body. There was a teasing glimmer in her eyes, as she let her tongue flick out to swipe little licks at my phallus.

"Sweet . . . ah! Mercy!"

Maxine tipped my dick closer to her, chuckling as she titled her head side-on to let her lips slide along either side of it. "Mm, aren't you enjoying this?" she asked when she backed up a bit. "I know I am!" With that, she swiped a long lick from the base to the crown, making a light slurping sound, like she was licking an ice cream cone.

The whole bit made my toes curl! "Damn it, lady! You're a hot lil' tease," I panted.

"That's the general idea," Maxine murmured, mouthing my dick as she brought her other hand around to lightly manipulate my balls with feather-light scratches and soft rolls of her fingertips. Eventually, after a few more swipes with her tongue, she tilted the column of my cock back and slipped the crown through her lips to draw it in, inch by inch!

Moaning, I dropped my head back against the rock-surface, with my eyes squeezed shut against the sudden Universe of wet, sucking flesh that had enveloped me.

Turning my hands over, I gripped the damp floor of the grotto as I gently rocked upwards with each tug and pull of her mouth, while she made whip-flick licks along my dick's underside with the tongue. With every passing second, she was sucking me up to a fine climax, which I tried to hold off as best as I could.

When she started humming, the ripples of pleasure nearly made me pop the top of my head off, when-!

"*A-hem!*"

What the-?

"*A-HEM!* Excuse me, Sir!"

Snapping my eyes open, I peered ahead . . . straight into the upside-down face of someone wearing a bartender's uniform!

Holy Hell!

I tried to turn over, but Maxine had my lower body and legs pinned to the grotto floor. Twisting as best as I could, I finally got my viewpoint skewed about, in time to realize the extent of this . . . now rather sticky situation! The second waterfall was gone, revealing it had been a 'curtain' for the back of the grotto. This was now opened up to a small, in-ground pond, which was the decorative backdrop to one of the hotel's barrooms!

In fact, the only saving grace for both me and my girl at that moment, was the fact this particular bar wasn't full. The only living soul in it was the bartender — who was standing there, scowling with his arms crossed — and, to my further embarrassment, a man and a woman sitting across from this backdrop, on the other side of the bar top!

"Ahh . . . ?" I tried to form some sort of apology, but wasn't doing a very good job; due to the fact Maxine was doubling her efforts to bring me off just then!

The bartender's frown deepened. "Sir! Do you mind!?"

There was a chuckle from the couple behind him.

Gasping, even though I was mortified, I couldn't fight for long against Max's persistence and talent. "Ah, actually . . . chum, but I really don't at the moment!"

"Oh, don't stop on our account!" The gal — a brown-haired lady in her twenties — said tartly. This got a nudge and a laugh from the guy sitting next to her.

I would've said something more, at least to forestall the flaring anger in the barkeep's face but, at that point, I was literally floored when Max did. I can't say WHAT, but it was enough to make me drop back down onto my back as my orgasm hit, full-force! Groaning out of control, I bucked up and let go; m y only conscious thought just then was listening to the the subtle swallowing motions around my dick and the gasps from the unplanned trio of witnesses behind me.

Eventually, my body stopped ripping out and,

with my climax still tingling through my legs, I reached down to pull my trunks up and sit up quick to shield Maxine from the peeping eyes in the bar. "C'mon!" I mumbled, scooping up my lover as I rose to my feet to beat a retreat through the front of the waterfall. Behind me, I hear the burst of excited chatter by the young couple, followed by some harsh, loud words fired off by the bar-keeper!

Hell! Hope we can get to our room before the house-dicks get out here!

Well, we did make it out of the pool — even with Maxine laughing all the way, and despite having to grab our stuff and wrestle with the pool deck doors! — and back into the elevator before any of the staff came running to catch us. All the way back up in the elevator, Maxine was grin-ning like a cat with its whiskers in the cream ; which was accurate, considering what she did to me back there in the waterfall!

Back in our robes, and with everything back in place, I just looked at her for the longest time. "Cripes, doll! Did you realize-?"

"Well, not at first!" Maxine said, still smil-ing as she licked her lips — a satisfied gesture, if I ever saw one! — and leaned back to regard me. "I . . . take it you're not happy?"

Snorting, I said, "With your skills with a skin-flute? Hell, do you even have to ask?!" I shook my head. "Maxine, did you realize we were practically about to screw in the middle of bar?"

Maxine cocked her head. "That'd be kinky for me . . .but, a first nonetheless." She stared back at me, her smile fading a bit in the face of my upset expression. "What's wrong, Bud?"

"Considering we were practically performing for a private audience there," I said, "I'm just a little unnerved, doll!"

"Oh, come on! What happened to the guy that was giving me a good romping fuck in the alley the other night?"

"Maxine! That was just the two of us, then!" I crossed my arms, and looked away from her. "Geez! I'm surprised we didn't have a few of the house-dicks there, waiting until we were finished."

Maxine stepped away from the wall and moved up next to me, leaning in so she could look up into my eyes. "John, I honestly didn't know about that cave opening up in the back like that," she said, every word colored with sincerity. "Had I guessed . . . well, I like a little adventure, but seriously? I would never put you purposely in an embarrassing position like that!"

I just snorted softly. "You could've checked, when you hid in there."

She nodded. "True but, even with that little nit, you have to admit-." She reached out and touched my cheek, making me focus on her. "That was a pretty hot blowjob, hm?"

Cooling off, I shrugged and murmured. "Curled my toes."

With a slow smile, she scooted closer and wrapped her arms around me. "I'm glad . . . I'd hate to think my lip-service isn't up to your expectations, lover."

Hell, I really couldn't stay mad at her. I mean, we did get away, and hopefully that bartender wouldn't press the issue-? I cut myself off and wrapped Maxine in a hug. "Doll, you've never disappointed me," I said. "Not once."

"Good," she purred softly, nuzzling into my chest as the elevator cab came to a stop. Looking up, she nudged me and added, "Think you can return the favor? Only . . . in a more private setting?"

With a smile, I scooped her up into my arms and chuckled. "Maxine, that's the only way I prefer it; one to one, with a *captive* audience!"

With a light shriek of "Ooo!", Maxine clung to me as I stepped out of the elevator and carried her down the hallway, back to our room . . . and just so you know, I gave her a command performance, with many encores too!

STEPHEN R. SOBOTKA

TWO OF A KIND

4. - Trouble

I got worked, but what's worse than that
Just as he was leaving he tipped his hat
Then he laughed and said,
I'm sorry bout your luck
When he walked out the door
he got hit by a truck

— "Aces & 8's", Uncle Kracker

TWO OF A KIND

The following night I half expected the hotel's management to come knock ing on Maxine's door to bring a lot of flack against us for our lil' voyeur show, back in the bar's grotto. Both Max and I were sort of on eggshells around the hotel staff, and I did get cornered by one of the night-shift security staff when I was making my way through the casino.

I thought it was going to be trouble, but the guy turned out to be a good sport about it all. Seems some previous guests did some things that were . . . well, a lot wilder than giving head in the late-night bar's fountain! I think he also bought the whole 'newlyweds' line I spun for him as well . . . with some people, I can't always rely on a good 'push' to make them change their tune some-times!

After dodging that bullet, things seemed to calm down a bit for the two of us and the next few nights ahead looked to be pretty well set for us to relax and enjoy our time together. Though Max still had her post-convention work to deal with, we both agreed that we'd met up after most of it was done by sunset . . . and then, the night was ours!

Until then, I had some things to keep me oc-cupied and . . . well, after all, this is Vegas. With a gal like Max and no worries to bother us, what could possibly go wrong?

Little did we know, and brother this was one time I wish I'd been more prepared for what hap-pened to us that night . . . .

Now, I'll give the 'Rock credit. When they tell you they can run a mean table for poker, they mean it!

I'm not talking about the typical stuff out on the main floor, like that Pai-Gow, Caribbean-Stud bull-puckey! I'm talking about the type of game you can only play in a back room; with a cluster of better-than-above average players, a bunch of deep products and a thirst for high-stakes, good drinks and . . . well, you get the picture.

That night, I got a line on a game being run

that sounded promising to me. So, I put the word into one of the cuties on the staff, who got it into the ear of the back-table boss and in due time, I was in.

Set up in one of the private rooms, the game was between some pretty experienced hands. I intended to bring my 'A'-game, and for at least a few hours I looked forward to having a good time with the cards.

In on this particular game with me were four other players . . . starting with a Spanish fellow, Caesar. He was a thin-made guy with a leather jacket, practically reeking of cheap cologne and a Cuban cigar. Slicked-back hair and a beard, he looked like a reject from a bad, modern-day mob flick . . . believe you me, I know what a member of 'the family' really looks like! He liked to bluff a lot, but he had some skills if the chips next to him were any indication.

Then we have this sandy-haired Australian bloke; Steve, I think he said his name was. One of those semi-serious players, but more of a tour-ist-y type, if the really bad fashion sense he had was anything to go by, what with his khaki suit and flower-print shirt. He even had that signature accent, peppered with a few 'G'days' and the like. He had a leather hat on, and a tall glass of beer with him.

I preferred him over the Spaniard, since he took his loses with a smile, at the least.

Rounding us out were a pair of local guys I'd seen around the casino floor these past nights. Not really good with their names, but then again they didn't play with any sort of remarkable skill or style. I didn't expect much of a challenge from them anyway.

The game of choice for us? Poker, with fast hands, quick-thinking and a steady rotation of drinks, bowls of pretzels and winners and losers. In one series of hands, Steve had managed to trump the both of us with a handy four-of-a-kind. I got him back later with a hard-played pair of pairs — tens and sevens — only to get zonked by Caesar when he bluffed his way to a tidy sum on a high ace.

Just another night for your average gambler, naturally. We all know there's no real animosity between professionals. Still, none of us wanted to leave holding the empty end of the sack, so to speak.

We started out pretty much even, all with a decent amount of chips all around, and had progressed through several rounds and turns as the night wore on. By the time I looked up to notice the time, we'd gotten so far along with the game, we just started just letting the pot ride, no matter who won the hand.

That particular moment, there was a hefty amount of winnings in the middle of the table. Whoever won the next hand or so was going to come away with a good haul tonight, so it was time the three of us got down to the nitty-gritty.

The current pot was looking as big as life in the center of the green felt swath between us. I got the feeling that this was going to be the final hand for the night . . . and the big question, naturally, was who's turn was it to have Lady Fortune on their side: me, the Spaniard or the fellow from Down Under?

"Right, mates," our friend Steve grinned, tipping his hat up over his forehead, looking at the two of us with his light-blue eyes. "Ante up, an' good luck! May the best man win it all!"

The Spaniard scowled - he had a habit of doing that when he got serious; it made his dark complexion even more gruesome, in my opinion. With one hand, he tossed a hundred-dolalr chip into the pile. "I scarcely think you or our sallow friend there, hardly qualify . . . but, we shall see, eh?"

I just shrugged. "Can't wait myself," I said, putting my ante in.

The dealer turned back from preparing a new 'shoe. Cute kid — blonde and bright-eyed, though no where near Maxine's class of looks! — in her hotel uniform and vest. She'd been watching all the action during the entire time, and it was clear from the look on her face she was expecting this last hand to be a hum-dinger.

"Your call on the rules, sir," she prompted,

putting her hands on the table to wait for my say-so.

"The game's Five-card draw, simple and straight. No Hi-Lo and no wild cards. Best hand takes all," I said smoothly.

Both of my opponents looked surprised. "Straight turn of luck, mate?" Steve rubbed his chin, then shrugged. "Fair dinkum, I'm game!"

Caesar frowned, clearly expecting something with a bit more kick this time around. "Deal the cards, *muchacha* . . . and let's get this over with!"

I made a mental note to tell Steve, after the game was over; never act glib around a Spaniard, in the future. When they lose more than their wallets can handle, they tend to not play so nice.

The cards were dealt out, the dealer's movements quick and efficient as she tugged them from the card-shoe to flick them across to each of us. I scooped up mine, just as quick, and tried to maintain a cool face as I weighed my options versus what could be gotten, when the draw came around.

"Right," Steve said, pursing his lips as he walked his eyes over the cards in his hand. "Since it'll cost big bikkies to win out, I'll start this show." He fingered his small stack of remaining chips idly, just before trapping half of them between his fingers. "Three-hundred on the jump, boys!" He flipped them into the pot.

Caesar stared hard at his cards, looking like he'd set them on fire his eyes were so intense!

Eventually, he swiped one of the smaller stacks of chips beside him, and threw them into the middle. "I will see you, *cazador del cocodrilo*, and raise the bet one-hundred more!"

Steve made a pinched face. "Oy, knock that garbo off, mate. I told you, I work in big business," he said crossly.

"Forgive me," Caesar said, chuckling as he took a drag on his stogie. "Well?" He looked at me. "Your move."

I didn't flinch, picking up five chips and popping them into the pile. "I'll see that, and raise you one-hundred more."

Whistling, Steve made another glance down, before he added a few chips to the pot. "I call ya, chum."

"Call," the Spaniard muttered, putting his contribution in.

The dealer made a quick sweep of the table. "Cards, anyone?" she asked, looking to the Aussie first.

"Hmm, gimme two, darlin'," Steve replied, plucking two cards to give back to the dealer. "Treat me nice, eh?" he added, giving the girl a wink.

Before the new cards had even landed, Caesar slapped three cards down and slid them over towards the dealer. "*Tres*." As he got his three, the look on his face shifted from dark to light - like someone plugged a light bulb under his kisser.

He looked at me, a challenge in his eyes.

"Sir? Any cards?" the dealer prompted me.

I didn't mince words. "Just two."

As I got the cards, I peered down briefly at their faces, then set them down in front of me without another word.

Steve just scratched his head, looking at me and then at my face-down cards. "Hey, ain'cha gonna look at them?"

"Must be good for him, not that it matters," Caesar said smugly. "If Lady Luck *knows* what is good for him, eh?

I didn't bother to rise to his jibe. Brother I hated playing spoilsports like Caesar; they were either overconfident, or got too sore when the cards didn't turn in their favor!

"Okay, gentlemen . . . last round of betting, before we get to see your hands." The dealer looked at the Spaniard. "Would you care to start, sir?

Caesar smirked, before he ran his fingers along the last stack under his hand. "Why not make this last round interesting, gentlemen?" He clutched his chips and dropped them into the pot. "I go all-in."

That drew a whistle from Steve. "Coo, that's a bit too much of a tuckah for me to handle!" He palmed his cards and pushed them over towards the deal. "I fold," he said, before nodding at me. "Good luck on ya, mate."

"He will need it, I am certain of that!" Caesar chuckled.

I didn't even blink as I pushed the last of my chips into the pile. "All-in."

That made my cigar-smoking friend over there grin all that much more.

"Very well, gentlemen," The dealer said. "May we please see your cards?"

Caesar flipped his cards over one by one, drawing out a long drag before letting the smoke seep out in a curtain in front of his face. Leering at me, he chuckled darkly. "*Dos pares. . . ¡siete y* Jacks, *mi amigo!*"

Steve hissed a breath, seeing twin sets of seven and Jacks in front of the Spaniard. "Aw, I can't believe I bowed out for that!"

"We have two pair showing," the dealer said. "Sir, may we see your cards now?" she asked me.

I arched one eyebrow, before I slowly reached for my hand. "You do a good bit of bluffin', *mi compañero.*"

"*Gracias.*" Caesar nodded, leaning up with his hands out, eager to scoop up his winnings.

"However," I stopped him with that one word. "I don't think you bluffed me that good, chum."

"*Por que?*" He looked at me, his face darkening.

With that, I exposed my five cards, and smiled back with a chuckle. "Three of a kind, with a pair."

I expected him to get angry — well, sore certainly, or screaming pissed off at the most. — but, he took one look at my cards and . . . to the surprise of us all, he went white as a sheet. "*¡Madre de Dios!* " His eyes went wide like silver dollars, and his hand shook as he lifted it to make a rapid sign over his heart. "*¡No! ¡La Mano Del Hombre Muerto!*" With that, he staggered away from the table, tumbling back over his chair in the process, before he could turn and bolt for the door; running out of there like he'd seen me pull a pistol!

The dealer and everyone else watched with wordless shock at the spectacle in front of them.

Having never moved since I showed them my cards, I looked at them and shrugged. "Guess I win, then."

The dealer nodded, quickly regaining her composure. "Congratulations, the pot is yours, Sir. Over twenty-five thousand dollars," she said.

I shrugged and reached out to snag a good chunk of the chips. "I'll just take what I came in with," I said, nodding at the rest of the pile. "Just divvy up the rest with these guys, okay? No sense in everyone walking away empty-handed."

At that, Steve whistled low and smiled broadly. "Man, that's a right deal, chum! Thanks for the payback!"

I just tipped my hat. "Consider it professional courtesy," I said. Besides, I'd had my fun, and I already had my room and board worked out prior, so . . . no sense in being greedy, right?

"Still, I gotta wonder," Steve said while the dealer divided the remaining chips. "What got into that bloke? He acted like someone shoved a Mamba in his face."

I had to laugh at that. "You don't know your poker history, do you?"

"Why's that, mate?"

Seeing the dealer grin — she knew what I meant! Smart cookie! — I pointed at my cards, which were still laying flat on the table. "I figure our Spanish friend was highly superstitious, considering the cards I had: two aces over three eights," I said.

"Come again?" The Aussie stared at the cards.

"A similar hand was held by a famous shootist — one named Wild Bill Hickock — just before someone shot him dead," I said. "Since then, it's been popular to call this particular combination of cards 'The Dead Man's Hand'."

At that, Steve's eyes lit up with comprehension, and he started to chuckle as he looked at me. "Oh, Crikey! No wondah he got all flustered! Probably figured you were gonna get zapped, and him bein' across from ya-."

"Well, whatever the case," I said quickly, hoping to avoid a more morbid turn of this conversation, "he's gone, we're still here . . . and, with that, I've got a redhead to meet up with, so thanks for the game." Standing up, I collected my take and nodded to the dealer. "Here, kid," I said, flipping her a one-hundred dollar chip.

"Thank you, Sir!" she said, smiling. "It was a treat to watch you gentlemen play."

"Any time you have a table free, I'll be glad to entertain . . . though, hopefully without someone who's too superstitious," I said, giving everyone a wave as I headed for the door. "Take care, now."

Once I made it back out into the casino-proper, I took a quick stop by the cashier to get my take of chips transferred back into cash, before heading back to the hotel lobby.

Hopefully finished by now, Maxine was supposed to be back from her business meetings for most of the day, and considering the mood I was in — winning always puts a guy in a good mindset. — I wanted her and me to celebrate with my winnings, somehow.

In spite of all the action, the lights and general noise around me, I managed to get clear from the floor and make my way out into the short stretch of marble-floor space that connected the lobby to the casino.

I found a couple of chairs set between two decorative columns. Considering it would be easier to wait for Max than go hunting for her, I plopped myself down in the nearest one and, with a slow drift down into the padded leather I stretched my legs out to relax and watch all the comings and goings of the casino. With people dashing in, couples strolling by, tourists chattering in groups, and poor souls who looked like they just lost their proverbial shirts staggering out, it made for a pretty full canvas.

So engrossed in people-watching, I didn't catch the sound of footsteps behind me . . .but I sure as hell didn't miss the pair of slim hands slipping down over my eyes, or the voice that purred next to my ear! "Guess who."

Breathing in, I chuckled briefly when I got a whiff of her scent, then I tilted my head a bit, and frowned as if thinking hard. "Um, gee . . . how many guesses do I get?"

"You really shouldn't need to guess," her voice said; that familiar tone curling around my ear warmly. "Though I guess I can be a sport. Three."

"Well then," I said with a grin. "Could it be, Lana Turner?"

"Mm, well she's got some really great legs — not as good as mine, though — but, no," the voice drawled. "Guess again!"

"Ah, damn," I mumbled with a touch of a sulk in my smile. "I always did like her gams. Well, hm . . . not her? How about Grace Kelly?"

"That's a good choice! Still wrong, but a good choice," she said with a chuckle. "Last guess,

Bud!"

"Well, I'd better get it right then!" I tapped my chin with one finger. "Well, it's not Olivia de'Haveland, then . . . ." I whipped one hand back around, coming in contact with side of a firm bottom, encased in a tight skirt. "A-ha! It's got to be my favorite red-haired gal!"

With a laugh, Maxine uncovered my eyes and leaned over my shoulder to place a smooch on my cheek, "Good guess, lover!" She hummed as she planted a second kiss on my lips, wrapping her arms around my shoulders from behind. "Miss me?" she asked, pulling back a bit.

"Nah, I think I can spot you pretty good, doll," I quipped, grinning as I turned in the chair to face her. Looking every inch like a successful business woman in her navy dress suit, cream top and pumps, I couldn't help but give her an appreciative wolf-whistle. "You look damn hot, doll!"

"Flatterer," she said, all warmth as she leaned back. "Thank you, though these heels are killing me!" She reached down to remove one, rubbing the arch of her foot with a sigh. "That feels good!"

"Sounds like you had a good night, in spite of having to wear those heels. How did it go?"

Propping herself up with her hands on the seat's wide back, Maxine nodded with a smile that was all rich-satisfaction. "I've been speaking with no less than three new distributors. Pretty much a full-dose of boardroom gymnastics, but I managed to get them to sign up some lucrative deals with *Bondage Babes*," she said. "After that, I talked with my boss and I'm pretty much the flavor of the month with everyone back East. If things work out, I'm going to be sitting pretty as far as my future income goes!"

Smiling back, I said, "Sounds like you did great to me!"

"Believe me, it looks great . . . at least on paper," she said with a note of triumph, before she let her shoulders sag and she groaned. "But I am so worn down now . . . ugh! I could so use a rest!"

"Aw, you're not up for some celebratin', doll?" I pulled out the wad of cash from my jacket pocket — tucked neatly into my money clip — and showed it to her. "I made some good bread myself at the tables tonight."

Maxine smiled. "Then you can treat for dinner . . . but only after I get to treat you, first."

"Oh? What exactly did you have in mind?"

"Ah-ah . . . that's my surprise, but you can help me out a little bit," she said.

"How?"

Reaching around me, Maxine fingered the money clip and plucked several bills from the top of the stack. "This is good, for starters," she said.

"Ah, now it comes out, Max! You just love me for my money!" I teased.

"Just for that, you talk to room service about

getting dinner sent up to our room, before joining me in the hotel spa in thirty minutes."

"The spa?" I arched my eyebrows.

"Sure! We're both in need of some relaxation . . . you're knocking them all off their rockers on the floor out there, while I'm toiling away in the boardrooms all morning long," she said with a grin.

"Aren't those places just for you gals?" I asked.

"Oh hardly! They don't just do manicures and facials," Maxine said. "They offer the full-treatment; spa showers, relaxing baths and even full massages!" She shivered a bit before smiling. "Always does me good to have my sore body worked over by a good pair of hands," she said, teasing me.

"I always thought I did a good job on that score, doll!" I snorted, looking hurt, but I couldn't make it stick.

"Aw, you're good with your hands, but sometimes it takes a professional to really work out the kinks."

I just chuckled. "You're never going to be rid of all your 'kink', Max." Even though I was a bit put off, I have to admit this talk was getting to me. "Still, all of this has me intrigued."

"That's the whole idea, lover," she said, grinning as she rose up. Eying the bills in her hand, she added, "Hope you don't mind, but I'll put these to good use, preparing for your surprise."

Standing up, I just shook my head. "Knowing you, it's going to be something I probably won't be prepared for."

"Aw," she cooed, stepping around to slip underneath my right arm, before she smiled up at me, while walking her fingers along my silk tie. "Even so, don't all my surprises please you, in the end, hm?" She pouted her lips before tracing one fingernail along my jaw. "Besides, you're really going to like this one, lover. That I promise."

Sighing, I just chuckled. "Okay, doll. If that's what you want, then I'm all-in."

With a nod, Maxine stretched up and kissed me briefly. "Good, now scoot. You've got to order our dinner, and go get a proper outfit for the spa." She left her hand on me as she stepped away, leaving a lingering touch before she was out of reach. "I'll be looking out for you, Bud . . . don't keep me waiting too long, okay?" The twinkle in her eyes was practically melting the air between us.

"I'll be there with bells on, doll." I promised, watching her go — and getting a good view of her hips-swaying walk in the process! — before I turned and walked off to find the concierge and get a good, three-course meal sent up to our room. Not exactly how I'd thought we'd celebrate, but hell! When Maxine has something in mind, your best bet is to just let it ride and enjoy it.

Getting dinner set up wasn't too hard to accomplish, really. Hell, I'd made a good amount of cash . . . and, all it takes is a few good greens in the right hands to get anything you want in Vegas!

After I made the arrangements with the front desk for dinner, I made a quick trip up to the room to get my trunks and one of the complimentary bathrobes — something all fluffy cotton, with the hotel logo on the front — before I made my way towards the side wing where the spa was kept.

The spa sat a little further along on the main floor, just beyond the hotel shops and restaurant; tucked in between two marble fountains, with an all-glass door front and shiny chrome accents all over. Even from outside, I could smell the scents of steam and exotic flavors floating in the air . . . kind of soothing, really . . . if you're into all of that aromatic-geedunk, anyway.

Stepping inside, I took a moment to look around the foyer. There was a comfortable-looking reception area — with a standing desk, some long couches against one wall, a glass-top coffee table and some feather-edged throw rugs underfoot — and warm, inviting lighting all around.

Behind the desk, a classy-looking dame with a brunette coif stood near a small computer monitor; wearing a tastefully-cut black dress, with a purple scarf and low heel shoes to match. She looked at me from over the tops of her thin, wire-frame glasses, her black eyes coolly taking in my old-world Chicago style. "Yes, can I help you?"

"Hi, um, I', supposed to meet someone here? Her name's Reynolds," I said.

The lady glanced down at a clipboard she held in one hand, before she smiled up at me and said, "Ah, yes . . . Mr. Walker. We were told to expect you coming along," she said. "Just one moment, I'll have your attendant take you back to your private room."

I nodded. "Sure," I said, standing there while she moved off through an open hallway. Private room, hm? Looks like Maxine's plan is getting better by the moment.

Not long after the receptionist left, a blond woman appeared in the hallway, paused to look around, before she saw me and walked briskly over to smile and ask, "Mr. Walker?"

"That's me."

"I'm Joanna, and I'll be at your service tonight," she said brightly, extending her hand to shake mine. Wearing a short-sleeved, pastel shirt, khaki shorts and boat-sandals, she looked like a lot of the gals I'd seen in some of the hotel's video ads on their in-house TV-channel.

I took her hand, shaking it in return briefly. "Nice to meet you, Joanna. I take it Miss Reynolds is waiting for me in our room?"

A flicker of something crossed her face, but she smiled in an apologetic manner. "I'm sorry, she had to step out for a few minutes, but she did tell me to have you go ahead and be in the room. Shall we?" She motioned towards the hallway.

Call me crazy but, for some reason when she said that, I got that crawling-roach feeling in my head. Still, what was there to worry about?

"Well . . . sure, why not? I guess I could start without her."

"Good!" Joanna turned to lead me towards the back rooms. "Just follow me," she said brightly . . . a little too brightly, at least the way I thought just then.

Moving down the hallway — lined with sealed doors and glass partitions — I couldn't shake that feeling! It usually cropped up when someone proved to be a serious threat against me, or when there was something rotten going on, out of plain sight. Still, Maxine had this all set up, so what if she had to step out for a bit? Walking along, I just shrugged . . . figure she's got some last-minute wrinkle to her little surprise, I guess.

Joanna finally stopped in front of a closed door near the end of the hall. Opening it, she ushered me into a richly-carpeted hallway beyond, directing me to one of the two doors in front of me. "Just step inside there, and make yourself at home! I'll be right back to get you started on your

. . . special treatment," she said.

I just nodded. "Fine, just let Miss Reynolds know where I am when she gets back, 'kay?"

The blonde paused; her smile faltering briefly before it slid back up to full-power. "Sure, Sir! Not a problem!" With that, she disappeared back into the main hallway.

Again, that funny feeling rose up. Crud, just what was setting me off!? Hell, I shouldn't be worried over anything! Maxine and I had some good times planned. Shaking it off, I stepped into the doorway on my left. I'd figure it out, soon enough, I guessed . . . but, still . . . .

Inside, I was presented with a neat little set-up: a massage table, a low bench with hooks for clothes, a private shower stall and a large Jacuzzi bath filling up one corner of the room. Sweet-looking, I had to admit. Wondered briefly as to what this was going to do to Maxine's travel expenses, before I put my bathrobe on one of the hooks and started stripping down to my skivvies.

I'd just hung my clothes up, and was belting my robe tight around my middle, when Joanna returned. Again, I caught something briefly about her expression — apprehension? — before she smiled and nodded. "Good, good! We've got a full session in store for you tonight, Mr. Walker; bath or shower, then a massage with therapy aromatics . . . Miss Reynolds insisted on giving you the 'treatment'."

I chuckled. "Sounds like Max, all right."

Joanna nodded briskly. "So, just step over this way, and we'll get you started right away."

"Shouldn't we wait, though?" I asked. "I mean, Miss Reynolds was supposed to be sharing this with me-."

"We shouldn't wait, Sir . . . I mean, considering the room is rented on an hourly basis," Joanna explained quickly. "Besides, I've left word for her with the receptionist, so she'll know where to find you."

Something wasn't right here. That crawling-roach feeling was back, stronger than before! I also got a brief whiff of Joanna's scent — hard to miss when you've got a nose as sensitive as mine. There was a slightly sour taste to it . . . like she was scared or something. I had put that down as her reacting to my general appearance, since I really didn't look like the picture of perfect health, being all pale and such.

At that moment though, everything just didn't click.

"Trust me, Mr. Walker," the blonde said firmly. "Everything's taken care of."

"Well . . . I guess, if she knows where I am-." Hell, I didn't like it, but I kept my poker-face on. "Okay, I guess I'm in your capable hands, then."

A look of partial relief crossed over her face. "Then would you prefer a shower, or perhaps a bath in our Jacuzzi?" She motioned towards it with one hand, smiling invitingly. "I guarantee the bubble-jets will give you a very relaxing bath!"

Well, when she put it that way, how could I refuse?

Joanna got everything ready: filled the bath with hot water, saturated with some light fragrant scent that I couldn't identify just then, along with some fluffy towels to dry off with afterwards. When I slipped in, she left me to simmer in the tub, switching on the bath's multitude of jets to stir the water into a burbling froth. She didn't leave though, making light comments while she puttered about the room to get the massage table ready for me.

All the while, I did try to relax. Sue me, but I really did try. Yet, a part of me was still niggling in the back of my brainpan, and the way Joanna kept moving around . . . she felt like a bird, locked in a cage with a hungry cat!

Nonetheless, I kept one eye aimed at the doorway, expecting Maxine to pop in at any moment to join in. Eventually, Joanna prompted me to leave the tub, using a couple of the towels to help me get dry. Again, I got this feeling she wasn't completely into this whole deal. Call me crazy, but it felt like she really didn't want to be up close to me. That threw up some major red-flags.

Wrapping one towel around my waist when I was mostly dry, I watched as Joanna moved to the padded massage table and moved some bottles of oil and other scented ingredients onto a small cart nearby. All the while, she kept glancing back at me, her face faltering from time to time before it slid back underneath her kilowatt smile.

Something about this didn't click right . . . and where the hell was Maxine now?

Just then, Joanna turned and stood before the massage table; her body titled back in a decidedly kittenish pose; chest up, hips back and legs stretched out so that she was standing on her toes. "So, are you ready to become putty under my hands, Mr. Walker?" Joanna asked, her voice attempting a sexy purr, even as I heard an undercurrent of timid fear coming from her.

"Um, I really think we should wait for Maxine," I said. I turned to reach for my bathrobe. "Maybe I'd better go check with the receptionist. She might have left a message-."

"No!"

The word practically left Joanna's lips at a dead shout, and the kittenish pose was gone in an instant. In fact, it looked like she was about to jump in front of the door . . . to stop me? From leaving? Now my head was buzzing!

"Okay, just what sort of deal is coming off here, lady!" I faced her and planted my fists on my hips. "Spill it, now!"

Joanna didn't fire back at me; she actually dropped to her knees and started pleading, saying, "Don't hurt me! Please! It wasn't my idea, really!"

"Idea?" I frowned. "Just what do you-?"

"It was his-!" She went hoarse, then swallowed as she got her voice back. "I mean . . . it was all Conner's plan, to get you two separated."

"Conner? Who the hell-?" I stopped, just as her words sank in. *To get us separated!?* "Maxine," I said softly, looking away towards the doorway before I wheeled back so fast, Joanna was cringing against the massage table. "What did you do to my girl, lady!? Where is she!?" I balled my hands into fists, but I really didn't need to threaten her, as she started talking . . . and boy, did she sing, but not the song I particularly wanted to hear!

"Conner s-said it was the best way . . . the only w-w-way, to keep you occupied while he got after her!" She blinked, going pale as a sheet as she continued talking. "He said y-your kind always have a thrall, or s-something, and the best way to s-set a tr-trap-?"

"A trap?" Some things were starting to click into place. Hell! I waved one hand and scowled, cutting off any further diatribe from her. "Let me guess. Conner's kidnapped Maxine, to use her against me . . . because he's twigged at to what I am, right?"

Nodding, the blonde looked like all the blood had drained down to her toes as she looked up at me. "B-because, y-you're a . . . a . . . !"

"I'm a vampire!" Great! Just what Maxine and I didn't need! I turned and quickly shucked both robe and towel, before reaching for my clothing nearby. "So, This Conner thinks he's going to trap a vampire, right?" I asked, not bothering to turn around. "Where's he taken Max?"

"H-he . . . he s-said he's got th-this place," Joanna said, her voice high and stammering from fear-stress. "H-he said h-he'd hide y-your thrall th-there-!" She shut her mouth, making a high-pitched squeak as I turned back to stare at her; my eyes dark and full of indigo fire.

"Get this, sister. Maxine's my girlfriend! Not some damn stooge from a Stoker-esque novel, get me!?" I started buttoning my shirt, making quick, savage motions with my fingers. When she nodded, her chin bobbing with jerking movements, I sighed and snorted through my nose. "Just where does he have her, lady? Talk fast!"

"I . . . I'm not s-supposed, t-to . . . I can't t-tell you!"

I growled. Damn it, I didn't want to do this but, time wasn't in high-supply just then. I stalked towards her, pausing when she scuttled backwards, eventually backing up against the near wall. "Lady, I'm in no mood for games, and frankly, you're not going to have a choice in the matter!" With that, I focused on her wide, unblinking eyes and 'pushed' . . . hell, as mad as I was, you could say I just battered her conscious mind aside and shoved my will into her skull!

She whimpered, clearly thinking I had meant to do something else — as she stiffened up like a priest's collar! — before she sat there, unmoving as I rooted around in her recent memories. Sheesh, this Conner had worked her into a tizzy, what with all the garbage I had to confront inside her head!

Eventually, I coaxed what I was looking for out of the mish-mash, and she said weakly, "At . . . some . . . old place . . . off of the main drag! Nearly a couple . . . miles from the . . . city limits!"

Jerking out of her head, I blinked and snarled, "Great!", before I reached for my pants.

Shaken, Joanna gasped and looked up at me; she looked nearly ready to faint, but I guess visions of what I might do to her if she did kept her from passing out. "Wh-wha . . . what did you-?"

"I didn't leave anything behind that you need to worry about," I said, jerking my pants back up as I scrambled into the rest of my clothes. Joanna just stood there — dazed and somewhat confused at my actions — until I was finished.

As I scooped up my overcoat, the thought hit me; *I can't go into this blind! Not if this kook's got in mind-!* I turned back towards Joanna, staring hard as she tried to curl back up into a ball. "C'mon, lady," I said firmly. "I need you to lead me to this dope, Conner."

That seemed to snap her out of her stupor.

"No! You can't leave here!" She didn't say that as a plea for her life, or mercy . . . It was a statement of fact.

"I can't, huh?"

"He . . . C-Conner told me . . . t-to-!" Her eyes locked on the doorway, stark against the pale complexion on her face. Another trap . . . it had to be!

I moved to the doorway and gingerly tested the knob. Nothing shocking, burning or the like, so I pulled it open and stared out into the hallway.

Nothing there . . . and a quick check left and right revealed no one lurking outside to nail me, either. I turned back and shot her a questioning stare.

"Well?"

Joanna managed to summon up the will to point at the floor.

Looking down, I almost had to laugh. The carpet outside the doorway was covered in tiny, white dots.

"Mustard seeds!" Whoever he was, this Conner bozo had done his homework on old vampire lore! However, I was at the end of my patience just then! Turning, I stalked over to Joanna, taking her by the arm — if not a bit urgently — and pushed her towards the door. "Come on!"

"B-B-but-!?" She shot a look down at the seed-strewn carpet. It was obvious she was shocked that a simple old folk-lore trick like this wasn't working.

"That sort of math never did strike my fancy, and I don't have any more time for such non-sense!" I pushed her further out into the hall. "You're going to get your coat, and show me where your boss took Maxine, now!"

After we got out of the spa — with some questioning looks from the receptionist — Joanna meekly directed me out of the hotel, to where a small car sat in the adjoining parking garage; little two-seater, somewhat dinged up but still running good, which was proven when she cranked it up after we clambered inside.

"You remember the way?" I asked. She nodded quickly. "Drive!"

Pulling out of the car-park, she turned off the main 'strip and started making her way up some side streets, heading west from the 'Rock. From where I sat in the passenger seat, it was clear that Joanna was in perpetual fear. I mean, she literally stank to High-Heaven, I could smell it so bad!

I knew she'd either bolt, or crash us if I did one thing to provoke her further. So, I tried to keep her calm . . . and the only way to do that was ask her questions. Well, I needed info on what I was up against, and she was my only source on this nut job that was threatening me and my girl.

"Tell me about Conner," I asked gently, keeping my voice as neutral as possible. "How did you get mixed up with him?"

She clutched the wheel hard, keeping her eyes fixed on the street ahead. "He just . . . he just came up to me, said he needed my help in g-getting you and your . . . girlfriend separated." She glanced at me, before turning off onto another street, accelerating quickly. "I thought it had to be some sort of gag, really . . . but, Conner was c-convinced you were-!"

"I get the gist, but what does he have on you, lady?" I scowled. "Did he threaten you, or . . . is he-?"

"No! I didn't know him until three days ago, when he first came up to me outside the hotel!" Joanna blanched at the memory. "He was all . . . creepy and, just, going on about how 'the devil-this' and how he n-needed my help to rid the world of . . . of evil, like you." She looked ready to be sick, this was affecting her that badly.

I just went quiet for a bit. Damn it, another wannabe Van Helsing, and from the sounds of it, a holy-roller to boot! "Great, just dandy!"

Joanna slid her eyes over, keeping tabs on me out of the corner of her eye as she turned the car and crossed two side streets. "Y-you're not g-gonna-?"

"What? Not going to do what?" I asked.

"K-k-kill m-me?"

"Who told you I'd do that? Conner?!" I snorted.

Joanna got a little bit bold. "Isn't that wh-what your kind does?"

Turning my head, I stared hard at her. "You people watch too many flicks these days," I muttered. "No, I'm not going to kill you," I said, trying to sound calm, even though my temper was on a short leash.

"But, Conner-?"

I snapped back, "Conner doesn't know anything about me, much less the difference between his own ass and a hole in the ground!"

Cringing, Joanna jerked the wheel, drawing a warning honk from a passing car in the opposite lane. "Sorry! Sorry, I'm-!"

I bit back on my anger, and held up one hand to forestall another frightened outburst from her. "Listen . . . no more 'Conner-told-me' stuff, okay? I just want to get Maxine away from him, and just leave it at that!"

"B-but, I-?" Joanna closed her mouth when she saw the glint in my eyes. "I'm sorry! I didn't wanna get mixed up in a-all of this, honest!"

"Look, just concentrate on driving," I said calmly, much more so than I had been before. "If I can stop this bozo from hurting Maxine . . . when its all over, you can tell your side to the cops."

She nodded. "You th-think you can stop h-him?"

Deep inside myself, there was a small part that had its doubts . . . but, the more rational side of me — along with the part that really cared for the redhead in danger — ignored it. "Lady," I said at length, "I'm going to give it a damned good try . . . that's for certain."

It was about a good half-hour's worth before we got to the outskirts of Vegas; out where there's more desert that buildings and, to be frank, not much more of anything else. Joanna and I didn't say much more along the way . . . she looked like she wanted to just pull over, bolt for cover and hope I didn't follow. Me? I just wanted to get to where Maxine was. *Hold on, doll! I'm not going to let that jerk get away with this!* I thought.

Eventually, Joanna slowed the car down as we got closer to a lone, two-story building off to the side of the road. A stone wall — knocked out and crumbling in a few places — enclosed what looked like a mock-cemetery, split by a short driveway, that filled the front yard. Pulling onto this gravel-strewn strip, Joanna let the car coast up nearly halfway along its length, before she braked and killed the engine. "Well . . . h-here you go! This is wh-where Conner said he'd be!"

From the first glance, I didn't like the looks of it . . . not one bit. This was clearly a roadside tourist-stop. I mean, it had all the hokey touches

— from the fake cobwebs in the windows, to the outlandish, ornate, wrought-iron fencing and all the bad puns on the tombstones littering the front lawn. There didn't seem to be any lights on inside . . . but, I got that crawling-roach feeling, big as life itself!

There was someone in there . . . and they didn't have my best interests in mind! I opened my door and grunted, swinging my legs out. "Get out."

"Wha-?" Joanna was terrified. "Not on your life!"

I peered back into the car. "Listen, you know what he's up to, lady . . . I'm not going into this half-blind! Besides, if Conner sees you're still around, he might change his mind about screwing around with my girl," I said.

"B-bu-but-!?"

"No 'buts', Joanna," I said firmly. "Don't make me 'push' you, like before . . . so, come out of there, now!"

Reluctantly, the blonde opened her door and slipped out to stand next to the far side of the hood. "B-but, you can't know what he's like!" She glanced at the haunted-house for a moment, before she turned a pleading expression towards me. "Please! Don't make me go in there!"

I thought for a second about just telling her to turn around, hit the road and never look back. After all, she was just as much an unwilling victim in this whole gig! Plus, if this kook had his hooks into her, she could give me away before I could act . . . possibly put my head on a damn silver platter for this Conner-guy.

Then, I had a quick flash of Maxine's face — smiling that saucy, sexy smile at me — before it turned into an expression of horror and fear. "Sorry, Joanna . . . I need your help, much as I hate to admit it," I said. "If Conner's hurt Maxine, you might have to run to get help . . . and, I can have you do that, if you're close to me." She started to say something, but I cut her off, jabbing a finger at her like the barrel of a forty-five caliber pistol. "Look, just so you know how this hand is being played out; you stick by me, keep quiet unless you see Maxine or Conner . . . and, if I tell you to run, you get the hell out and go get help." For emphasis, I added darkly, "Don't make me get inside your head and make you behave, understand me?"

Joanna nodded several times. "Y-yes, sir . . . I understand!"

With a sigh, I looked back at the spooky place in front of us. No telling what this Conner hand in mind. No telling if Maxine was even here, or still-! I smacked myself mentally. *Stop it! She's not dead yet!* I thought. How did I know? Same way I knew how to keep myself going on the streets near Roger's Park . . . trusted my gut.

I pointed towards the front of the building,

gesturing to Joanna with my chin. "Get going , lady. We've got business inside this creepy joint . . . with the head creep, himself!" *Hold on, Max!* I thought, wishing I had some other way to let her know help was on the way . . . .

TWO OF A KIND

5. - ...And A Hard Place.

I give . . .kerosine, divorces . . .
I light . . . angle wings, with torches!

I'm burnin'! Burnin'!

— "Gasonine", Kicking Harold

TWO OF A KIND

L ooking back, I know what I was about to do just then was all kinds of crazy! Getting set to step into a place I knew nothing about, with some loony-goon who didn't have my best interests in mind, and would most likely kill me if he got the chance-! Hell, for all I knew, this whole, abandoned roadside shack was just one big booby-trap.

With me being the biggest boob, if I wasn't careful!

Yet, for all of that, there was only one thing that was fixed in my mind . . . Maxine. She got mixed up in this circus, no thanks to me, and I wasn't going to give her up to this bozo's whims.

Not without a fight, by God!

Once inside, Joanna was just a bundle of nerves and shakes. I had to kinda be sympathetic . . . I mean, she was nearly blind in the dim-lit hallways, constantly clutching at the back or the sleeve of my overcoat as she stumbled along, trailing behind me for the most part while I made short work of the first floor's rooms just off the grand foyer. Most of these were empty . . . not a soul stirring, and no traps tripping when I stepped inside.

Truth be told, the whole house felt vacant . . . *felt* being the operative word, if you were just your average Joe, stumbling in on the place.

Then again, I'm far much more than 'average'.

One of the perks of being one of the walking undead — if you can call it that! — is that living flesh is damn easy to track down: each person emits a scent that's unique as a fingerprint, and with emotions riding high, it acts like a big, bright beacon. In a big empty place like this, it was easy for me to detect the only other living things other than Joanna.

Maxine.

Even with walls and junk between us, I could recognize that scent of hers. Spicy-sweet, but laced with a sour overtone of fear . . . and there someone else! A male, musky odor . . . but much closer! I stepped around a corner, and nearly ran into the haymaker that somebody pitched at me from out of the gloom!

Conner! I thought, ducking that wild swing. I didn't wait for this nut to step out into the clear; planting one foot as I turned into where I though their body would be, tossing a pair of punches that connected with a chambray-covered chest and a rock jaw lined with stubble.

A surprised grunt followed them, along with another ham fist that clipped my right ear and spun me around. Before I could recover, this gorilla literally had me wrapped up in a bear hug, trying to squeeze my ribcage like an accordion.

Gasping for a mouthful of air, I shoved the sharp point of my elbow into this guy's gut — got a satisfying feeling when I felt his breath whoosh out of him! — doubling him over so I could get one arm wrapped around his neck. Shoving him into a hip-toss, I kept his neck locked in the vise of my arm, letting my body's weight follow through with the motion that snapped his vertebrae like matchsticks!

With a shudder, the goon slid to the floor in a single pile, leaving me there with a slight sweat and a grim look on my kisser. Joanna watched it all from a spot nearby. She could speak as I reached down and turned the dead guy over into a patch of dim light. This Gorilla was ugly — scoop-shovel jaw, tiny eyes and a beat-in nose with a cauliflower ear — but, his face wasn't one I recognized.

"Is this Conner?" I asked Joanna.

Shaking her head quickly, the blonde said, "N-no! That's not him!"

Swell! I just killed one of his 'helpers', not the guy I was after. "Did he have any more bozos like this one around?" Joanna gave me a negative reply. "Did he even tell you what he had in store for me?"

Joanna said, "H-he just told me what to d-do at the hotel... then, j-just leave the r-rest to him!"

Perfect. Well, I knew this wasn't going to be a cakewalk! Grimacing, I tested the air again; I could still smell Maxine, but unless Conner was masking himself somehow . . . .

Hell! "Come on," I muttered to Joanna, motioning her to follow along.

"Where are y-you going?" Joanna asked me.

"The only place I can figure he'd be," I said softly. "After all, he wouldn't go through all this trouble, if he didn't want me to come find him, even if that goon did jump the gun a little!"

"B-but, shouldn't I-I-?"

"Just stay behind me, and keep quiet!"

Eventually, after leaving the main part of the mansion's front part, we both made our way down a long corridor, which ended at a pair of double doors leading into what had to be the mansion's main ballroom.

After all, I doubt the lady's powder room has two doors, as wide as I am tall, built panels of aged, dark oak wood which have a ton of ornate carvings on them, right? Besides, this was where Max's scent was coming from, strong as rum on my senses..

Wrinkling my nose, I just nodded as I cast a glance around the doorway for any traps or alarms. "Well, since he invited me-!" I stepped back, braced and put all of my weight behind one foot. Lashing out, I kicked one of the doors in, sending it crashing to the floor in a cloud of dust and a few splinters. Joanna cringed from the noise, but other than that, nothing moved or made a sound after the last clatter of wood against the floor faded away.

That's a good sign, I thought . . . or not.

Carefully, I edged my way around the door frame.

Behind me, Joanna tried to make herself small as she moved to stand by my side. I paused and motioned for her to stay put, before I turned back to face the rest of the room in front of us. Keeping with the creepy & kooky theme, the place was filled with stacks of unused tables and chairs — most covered with protective sheets or tarpaulins — along with a scattering of furniture that must've been in other rooms inside this place once. Someone must've moved them here to make space. Only a few windows along one side of the long room afforded me hardly any light to see with . . . turning the cloth-covered furniture and dusty relics into shadowy, forbidding shapes.

Well, not all of the room was in such a dim-array. A clear line of empty space, leading from the front door went clear to the small, raised plat-form of what had to have been a stage once. Flanked by two marble support columns, was a ring of lit candles on one side of the far end. This illuminated a lone figure, tied with their back to the right-side column, who wearing just a sheer set of lingerie and stockings underneath an open, baby-doll robe. Maxine!

"Doll?"

The figure raised their face towards me, a look of fear and recognition filled her face, while she tried to push a muffled sound through the cloth gag that had been tied between her lips.

I was relieved and mad all at once! The bas-tard must've snatched her when she was getting ready for me-! I shook myself, looking around for any sign of her captor. "Connor?!" I shouted, making the sound roll around the room like a thun-derclap. "Connor!"

From somewhere inside the room — hard to tell where, with all the sound echoing all around me! — a thick voice said, "Welcome, demon-spawn . . . Your thrall waits for you!"

I stiffened. Something in that voice . . . some-thing I recognized! "This is Conner, right?" I asked. "If so, then you've made a big mistake, kidnapping my girl!"

"Oh, you have feelings for this trollop?" A harsh burst of laughter followed. "Come, reclaim her if you dare!"

I gritted my teeth. *Sonofa-! Did he think I wouldn't jump at the chance to go to Maxine, cut away her bonds and . . . hell! Of course, that's just what he hoped I'd do!*

"Not yet," I said, getting a clamp on my temper as I stood there.

"Oh? Not so amorous or . . . inclined to come to her rescue yet?"

What is his angle? Is he expecting me to do something . . . well, more like a classical vampire? "Look, I don't want a fuss here, chum," I said, holding onto a slim thread of hope that this guy wasn't as around the bend as I feared. "Surely we can settle whatever beef you've got with me-?"

"I think not. Not when you are nearly inside my trap!" The voice sounded smug, before it turned chilly, saying, "Despite the failure of my accomplice to tempt you!"

I glanced back at Joanna briefly, before I said, "Sorry, but if you knew enough about me, you'd know I don't prefer blondes."

More laughter. "Ah, well . . . no matter! In the end, whatever strength you could have gained from her blood would have served you little anyway!"

That got my hackles up. Didn't this jerk care

about-? Something nagged at the back of my mind . . . something was fishy in Denmark. This clown seemed . . . almost, familiar? "I don't 'bleed' anyone, much less the innocent, you sumbitch!"

"There are no such things as innocents, where your kind are concerned! All of humanity are simply walking bags of sustenance, to the likes of you," Connor's voice shot back.

"You're a little behind the times, chum," I said, taking a measured step into the room. I could feel eyes all over me just then, but where was he hiding? "I don't treat every Tom, Dick and Sally as a food source these days."

"Oh, yes!" Conner's voice rose in mock-surprise. "I suppose you've lived on rats and cats and other tiny mammals for all of the years of your bastard existence, yes?"

Well, he wasn't too far off the mark, there. "More or less, yeah!"

"You are not a convincing liar, devil man!"

Something rustled above! I turned quickly, catching sight of a series of small, banister-lined balconies on the walls . . . could he be hiding there? "What makes you so certain, Conner!?"

"Because, I have studied the habits of vampires, and it is a known fact that only the pure blood of humans can maintain your immortal life!" There was a faint *tik-tik* sound, but Conner's next words masked the source of that sound: "But, that life is over! This is a proven ground, and I have labored hard these past few days . . . build-ing every means of giving you a most deserved death! God has decreed it, and I will carry on His will!"

Oh, swell. This guy could've come out of a bad matinee on a Saturday night! "Get this through that thick-brick you call a brain, chum," I said, peering up along the raised balconies in the gloom overhead. "God doesn't give a damn about my kind! Especially when he's got scum like you around! Now, let Maxine go, or else!"

"Your threats are as empty as your black heart, devil man," Conner said, steel in every word. "A heart I will relish stopping this night!

There was a sound of footsteps... from where, I couldn't pinpoint! I whipped around on sheer reflex, backing up a few steps into the ballroom to see if the dirt bag was on the balcony right behind me-!

He wasn't anywhere in sight!

I had to try a different tactic, before I had to resort to something more physical. "It doesn't have to be this way, Conner! I'll make you a deal; let Maxine go, and I'll leave Vegas, and never return-?"

"The only way you leave this place," Conner said; his voice cold, the laughter gone, "is through the gate of Hell!"

A split-second later, I heard the snap of a wire, or something under tension, suddenly released! I whipped aside, just as three, crude crossbow bolts slammed into the floor where I was standing! Skidding across the floor, I came to a stop in the deep shadows along the one wall. That was too close!

"Ah, I missed!"

"It'll take more than that to get me, Conner!" *Pull yourself together!* I told myself. *Can't let this dope rattle you! Maxine's the only thing that matters now... need to get her out of here!* Getting to my feet, I tried edging my way towards the stage by moving along the near wall; sticking to the shadows as I went.

"What's this? Are you trying to . . . avoid me?" Conner chuckled. "You cannot dodge all of my traps, devil man!"

"I can try!"

"Try or not . . . It will not matter, in the end!" Connor said archly.

I'd side-stepped about halfway across the hall, managing to avoid exposing myself out of shadow, when the whistle of something sailing through the air got my attention. Ducking, I felt something pass way too close to the back of my neck before it bit deeply into the wall.

I shot a quick look over my shoulder and gawked at the razor-toothed saw blade was imbedded there. *Shit!* Another whistle of air — lower this time! — made me shove off with one foot, forcing me to roll forward in the nick of time.

Two smacks against the wall where I'd just been, and two more saw blades joined the first one.

"Damn it!"

"Ah! I am getting closer, yes?" Conner chortled.

"Not close enough," I muttered to myself, scrambling towards the relative shelter of a dust-covered couch nearby. Ducking behind it, I slapped the floor in frustration. *If the entire place is staked out with booby-traps-?*

"What is wrong, devil man? Are we losing our unholy nerve!?"

Ah, hell! Now he was getting to be annoying with his constant taunting . . . and I was getting on my last nerve; unholy or not! *Concentrate, Bud!* I scrunched down, moving to the edge of the couch to peek around its near corner.

There, about twenty feet of open space separated me from the head of the hall, where the two support columns stood on the stage. A couple of wide-backed chairs, and a pile of thick, fur rugs blocked off the side-facing steps, limiting my options for access. The only way to get to Maxine was to get through a wide, clear space and vault over the front lip of the stage.

Not good! I started to move back towards the entrance, thinking to regroup-.

"Can't see the way to your harlot?" Conner's voice taunted me, now from somewhere behind me! "Here, let me LIGHT your way!" Something whizzed over my head, crashing into the floor with a crackle of glass and a rush of heat-!

Fire!

I jerked back, whipping around just in time to pull my legs out of the way of a spreading pool of a Molotov cocktail, but the flaming liquid splattered on the tails of my overcoat! *Geez! Didn't this asshole ever think of using an ounce of moderation!* I got clear, whipping off my coat to throw it down to stamp out the flames, only to hear two more Molotov's crash into the floor behind me. I cursed and moved as far from the fires as I could go. "Yes, burn! Burn, you bastard! Burn!" A spate of laughter rang out from overhead, echoing around the room as several more flaming bottles of gasoline shattered on the floor around me.

"I prefer to barbeque in the summer, you-!"

A sudden scream got my attention; Joanna!

With as many of the fire-bombs he'd thrown, Conner had managed to start a pretty-good sized blaze; the bulk of which had spread towards the doorway. In trying to dodge it, Joanna had gotten pinned against the one wall by the pool of flaming liquid.

"Damn!" I reached down to snatch up the topmost rug from the nearby pile and dashed over towards the screaming blonde. Risky! Against the flames, I was a sitting duck, but I couldn't let her get hurt . . . not by this sick bastard! Whipping the rug out, I beat it down onto the fire, hoping to smother enough of it so Joanna could get free.

Growling, I managed to knock out enough of the flaming liquid so I could reach over and pull her out from the wall. "I told you to stay put, but in this case-!"

"Look out!" Joanna shoved me back violently.

Off balance, I reacted by kicking her away with one foot planted in her belly. We both fell apart, just as a score of metal spikes rained down on the spot we were just standing on.

Whipping my head around, I looked for . . . there! In a spot of dim light, I caught sight of a shadowy shape against the wall; high up on another balcony. Holding a pair of crossbow-shapes, the figure quickly retreated into the shadows.

"I see you now, Conner, you rat bastard!"

"Only for a brief moment," he fired back from the darkness. "Soon you will see nothing but oblivion!"

"Not damn likely," I said sharply, getting to my feet. "I'm putting a stop to this fracas, right now!"

"Determined, to the last, eh? Come! Stop me, if you dare! Seeing you fail, will just make my holy victory all that more sweet, in the end!"

Seething, I started to head in his direction, when I heard a muffled cry, off to my right. *Maxine!* Looking over, I could still see her tied to the column; so close I could see the silvery tracks of fresh tears on her cheeks.

"Hold on, doll!" I stepped around the couch to make my way towards her, when something slammed into my side, knocking me across a good segment of floor space, before I rolled to a stop against one of the overturned tables! Before I could get my wits back, two hands latched onto the front of my shirt and hoisted me bodily off my backside. I kicked out, but got a knee driven into my breadbasket, followed by a solid, clubbing blow against the back of my head!

Hell! Either Conner was finally taking this into his own hands-?!

"Sorry, you bastard spawn," Conner said, his voice echoing down through the ringing in my ears. "It will not be so easy to reach your red-headed thrall!"

Shit, there was another goon helping him! A blow to my side — someone's foot taking an extreme dislike to my ribcage! — send me rolling away with a cry of rage-touched pain! I got a glimpse of a tall, thick-set figure in black, before another booted-foot connected with the side of my head.

"Good, yes . . . very good!" Conner sounded closer; clearly coming down from his hiding place to exhort in my misery. "Crush him! Do not give him a second to react!"

Trying to rise, I felt the goon wrap one hand around the back of my neck, raising me up so he could rain a series of punches on my face, chest and shoulders; each blow feeling like an iron hammer, causing a new burst of pain to jangle my nerves.

Somewhere behind me, I could hear Joanna's fear-filled whimpers, as well as the muffled cries from Maxine. Knocked as loopy as I was, I couldn't make my legs work. If the goon hadn't kept hold of me, I'd be dropping to the floor like a wet sack.

Through the haze threatening to wrap my head up, I could feel a line of wet along one cheek — one punch had cut the skin near my temple — and smell the scent of my own blood filling my senses .... which were getting fuzzy as my brains rattled around inside my skull. Damn it! If I didn't act fast, Conner's words were going to become true!

When the goon stopped slugging at me and gave his knuckles a breather, I marshaled what wits I had left and put all of the focus I could muster. As he pulled me back up to start another round of blows, I reached up like I was trying to ward him off.

"You're goin' down, punk!" he growled.

While he grappled with my one hand, I snapped the other one around to grasp his head, holding him still as I whipped my head up and shoved my kisser towards him; getting within an inch of his bulldog-shaped face.

"Fuck off!" I "pushed" . . . no, scratch that! I practically rammed my thoughts into his head, shrugging off any sort of concern as I bludgeoned his mind with every ounce of mental strength I had. The effect was like he'd taken a running start and slammed his skull against a brick wall. He literally shot backwards, his body tumbling backwards, ass over elbows, before he landed in a starfish-sprawl on the floor.

I didn't pause to pity the bastard. Before he could recover, I charged up and aimed the point of my foot with his exposed neck. There was a sick sound as flesh and cartilage gave way . . . a soggy sound of air being sucked down his damaged windpipe, then a gurgle as he fell down for the count, after I snapped another kick against the side of his head!

Felt like kicking a bowling ball! Still, he was out of the picture . . . now, I had to get back to-!

BLAM!

A hot spike of pain lanced through my left shoulder! The front of my shirt blossomed dark crimson, as the lump of thirty-eight caliber lead made its exit; the force of the bullet's passing twisting me around, forcing me to drop to one knee as I reached up to grab at the red stain.

Hissing, I snapped my eyes up-!

"That, will be quite, enough from you."

The first thing I locked my eyes on was the still-smoking muzzle of the gun; following the barrel back to where the hammer sat, unmoving until a fat thumb reached around and pulled it back to the fullstop. Following with my eyes, I stared back up the back of the hand holding the gun, up the arm, clad in a dark shirt sleeve, over a broad shoulder . . . and into a dark, scowling face; wreathed with long, unkempt black hair, stubble-dotted cheeks framing a pair of fat lips, a hooked nose and a pair of black eyes beneath the single, bushy line of an uni-brow.

Conner. For the life of me, I just knew I'd seen his mug somewhere before . . . but-?

"I . . . I know you."

"Not intimately, monster, but yes you do," Conner said. "You only were none too careful with your unholy trysting the other night, before you were carried beyond my hands by a taxi."

Suddenly, it hit me: The goon who bumped into me and Maxine, after we had . . . in the alley! "You . . . sumbitch!" I hissed, pressing harder against the spreading stain under my shirt.

"Seems you are not so proof against bullets, hmm?" Conner asked smugly. "Even though I could not afford ones of pure silver, it seems common lead can suffice to injure your kind!"

Wincing against the pain in my shoulder, I snarled and started to rise. "Just . . . give me, a minute-!"

"No, you stay put!" Conner's thick body shifted, so I could see past him, where he had his

other arm extended out towards the column behind him and his hand, which was holding a long
knife, pressed up against Maxine's exposed neck!

Shit! I stopped moving.

"Ah, so the demon can comprehend what will
happen if he tries to . . . act the hero? Good,"
Conner said, his face twisting with his cruel smile.
"Keep your hands where I can see them, if you
please?!" He kept smiling as I willed my hands
to stay in place. "A move, any move in a direction that does not meet with my expectations . . .
well, let us say, it will bode unfavorably for your
trollop, yes."

Understatement of the year, really. "All right
. . . what now, chum? You've got us both, but you
can't kill me without letting your guard down,
and you've got to know . . . killing her, will be
the worst mistake you'll ever make!"

Conner nodded slightly. "That is a mistake I
will not be making, hm? Not unless I wish to never
see your blackened bones left out in the sun," he
said. "I will kill you, devil-man."

"How? You're at a Mexican stand-off here!"
I had to think . . . had to work past the pain, the
blood smell. I needed an opening, somehow, to
get Maxine out of danger.

"Unfortunate for you, I have the means to
hold you at bay," Conner said, his eyes flashing
briefly as he looked over to the side. "You!
Woman!"

From the side, I heard Joanna's voice rise in a squeak. "Me!?"

"Come here! Now, or I will shoot you myself!" Conner snapped a look at me. "I have more than enough bullets to do so, and still finish you off!" He didn't make the gun move an inch. "No funny ideas, yes?"

I knelt there, still as a headstone.

Walking past me slowly, Joanna looked up at him, then over at me with fear-filled eyes.

"You need not fear this damned beast, woman! Now, move!" Conner snapped. As quickly as she dared, Joanna scooted across the floor to stand a short distance away from him. "Here," he said, nodding to where he was holding the knife on Maxine. "Take hold of this and do not remove it from her throat." As Joanna moved to comply, he added, "If he moves before I am done, kill her."

Joanna stared at Conner's face in shock. "K-kill her?"

At that, Conner barked harshly, "What, are you dumb between your ears, woman?" He reached out and forced her hand up against Maxine's neck, making both women wince as he pressed the blade in close. "You will do as I tell you to do, or by God, I will show you the true meaning of FEAR!"

I watched him there, grinding my teeth. Just hold on, I said to myself, more for Maxine's benefit than for myself. Geez . . . just give me an opening. Just one . . . and this clown would pay for this night! Believe you me.

When Joanna was sufficiently cowed, Conner turned to regard me, his gun hand never moving. "Now . . . devil-man," he said, reaching into his coat as he grinned like a shark, "I shall prepare you for your last moment on this good Earth." His hand emerged, removing a battered looking piece of wood, shaped like a cross, with one end sharpened into a point. "After I send you to Hell, I will purify this place with your funeral pyre!"

Think fast, John! I thought. *This bozo's not going to give you another chance!* Glancing quickly at the two women behind him, I knew what I had to do! Trouble is, I needed perfect timing. "Just one thing I have to know, Conner."

"Yes?" He stepped forward, eager for the kill, his full attention onto me.

"What's going to happen to Maxine, after I'm dead? I have a right to know," I offered. Perfect, he wasn't watching the girls as I started to pull power.

Conner snorted. "Still concerned for your little trollop? Fear not, devil-man. Once you are dead, she will follow you shortly thereafter, so as not to propagate your dammed influence on any other innocent souls!"

"So, even if I told you . . . she hasn't been turned by me," I asked, trying my best not to give away what I was trying to pull off. Behind him Joanna stiffed, as I slipped into her head; my will muffling her gasp, as I firmly took hold of her; mind and body and all.

"Hah! As If I'd believe a black lie from the likes of you," Conner snorted. "Your kind should learn in the end, it is the just and righteous people that will triumph over your unholy ways!" With that, he started to raise the cross.

"Ah, yeah... right!" I said, giving Joanna a final forceful push from my mind. Behind him, I saw Joanna flinch as I willed her hand to move the knife away from Maxine's throat.

"Farewell, you bastard!" Just as Conner lifted the make-shift stake higher to stab me, I sent one last pulse of power into Joanna, and she jerked her hand around, burying the knife into his right shoulder in one thrust! "AHHHH!"

On the heels of his pain-filled scream, Conner whipped around, wrenching the knife out of Joanna's hand as he backhanded her with the pistol; the blow dropping her with a cry and a whimper to the floor. "Bitch!" Conner reached up to fumble for the handle of the knife, when he suddenly realized what had happened! "Bastard!" he shrieked.

I surged forward, curling my fingers as I latched onto him like a cat on a mouse -- in this case, a rat! Conner barely had time to check my momentum as I lifted him off the floor like a sack of nothing. Trying to swing his pistol back around, I swatted at it savagely, sending the six-shooter sailing out of his grasp.

Surging forwards, I sent us barreling along the length of the room until we both slammed hard against one of the ballroom walls. With another yelp, he realized just how dire his position was. "N-no! Stop! H-how did y-you-?!"

For the first time that night, I saw fear in his face. I'm talking the kind of fear, when you realize that the big-rig's in your lane, and you can't avoid the rush as it barrels down on you!

I was going to enjoy this!

"Easy. I'm a vampire, remember?" Reaching up, I tore the knife out of his shoulder and tossed it aside. "I can seep into your soul... twist your heart until it bends to my evil whim, isn't that right?!" I got right up into his kisser, my eyes flaring wide as I hit him with all of the rage inside me. I hadn't been this angry in years, and I wasn't holding anything back. "Buster, I've got all the excuses in the world to kill you," I hissed through clenched teeth, letting my fangs show.

His eyes were like two tiny dots of black in a sea of white. He started shaking so much, I thought he was going to have a seizure. "N-no... p-please... have, m-mercy!"

"Mercy?" I barked, half-laughing at the tone in his voice. "Did you show *mercy* when I asked you to let my girl go? Huh?" I pulled him off the wall, only to slam him back against it, making the plaster crack. "No... you're on a mission from God, remember!? 'Kill all the vampires, an' let God sort 'em out', right!?"

Whimpering, Conner was scrabbling against my hand, trying to wriggle free.

"You really wanted to face an honest-to-living vampire, chum, so now you're going to reap the consequences!" With that, I reached up and snagged the edge of his shirt collar, jerking back to tear the cloth away, revealing his pale, pasty throat underneath.

At that, Conner really hit his panic-limit. Squirming around like a pinned frog on a gig, he cried at the top of his lungs, "No! NO! HELP! LET ME GO!"

With a growl, I pulled him close, getting right up against the side of his head as I got ready. "You're not going anywhere," I hissed. "Say 'g'night Gracie!'"

"NO!" Conner howled. I just let instinct take over, and sank my teeth into his neck.

The first gush of red over my tongue was like a sweet, tang-filled rush that had always been in the back of my mind. A part of me was always disgusted with this aspect of myself . . . but, the 'beast' — that part of me that had come around after the first time I had to feed — relished and loved this! This was rejuvenation . . . this was meat and milk to me now. *This was life!*

Bucking against my grip, Conner's cries were going softer as he felt his blood draining out of the wound in his neck. "No . . . s-stop . . . n-no!"

Growling in my throat, I swallowed, feeling the rush as the blood filled my throat and ran down towards my stomach. A warmth that no alcohol-rush could match spread through me. Hell, if I thought it was possible, you could say I could get drunk from this! Pulling back, I let out a cry of my own; bellowing, reveling in it as the sound echoed around the chamber. Damn, I was going to enjoy letting this bastard bleed . . . and after he was sucked dry-? I started to look around, the beast in me looking for more to sustain its rage.

That's when I turned my eyes on Maxine.

Still tied to the column, she had this look that spoke three things to my rage-clouded mind just then: utter horror, disgust, at what I was about to do... and lastly, a pleading undercurrent as heavy as concrete, begging me to stop.

Boys and girls, if you ever think there's nothing that can stop the blood-rage of a vampire... let me tell you, you're dead wrong.

At that exact moment, I was caught between two elements that were as powerful as anything else I'd experienced in my life. On the one hand, I wanted so badly to kill this mook! Put his light out for good, and save a lot of other people the grief of him coming into their lives. And yet, I was picking up this vibe from Maxine, that was literally pleading for me to stop before I committed an act that - in all hindsight - would make me no better than this piece of trash I was about to kill.

It took a lot of force of will . . . but I pulled back and shoved the beast I'd become back into its 'cage'; letting go of Connor as I closed my mouth with a soft click. Unable to stand, the wannabe vampire killer slid to the floor in a boneless heap; clutching his neck while still whimpering for his life.

Leaving him, I stalked towards Joanna, turning her over to check her out. She was out cold . . . a mercy, really. Didn't want to think of what she'd do if she'd seen-! Turning to look at Maxine, I could see she looked close to melting down into a full-blown panic; tugging at her ropes in a weak attempt to get away.

From me, I could imagine . . . but, right then, I didn't care much about her fear. Looking on the floor, I found the knife Joanna had stuck into Conner's shoulder — still coated with his blood. Scooping it up, I rose and moved to the side of the column, and made short work of the ropes. The instant she was free, Maxine nearly sagged to the floor, and I braced her with one arm to keep her upright.

"Hold on, doll. I got you." I hoped I sounded reassuring. God, she looked terrible! Her one cheek was a dull, faded red, which contrasted against her pale skin, along with her smudged make-up. Her nightdress had rips and some shot-through seams, and her wrists and feet bore rope marks, showing where Conner had her tied down too tight. She looked like hell, and I growled out of sheer reflex, and that made her shudder in the circle of my arms.

"Hey, hey, easy! It's gonna be okay, now," I told her, reaching up to pull the gag loose, allowing her to close her jaw for what seemed like ages. She gulped down several draughts of air through her abused lips, shuddering against my arms while she leaned away from me . . . and, considering I was bleeding from my shoulder still, along with traces of Conner's blood on my lips and chin, I shouldn't wonder that she was still terrified.

"Take it slow, doll, you're safe now."

"Bu-bu... B-Bud?"

"Just, take it easy," I soothed. "It . . . it's over, okay? I'm not gonna let him hurt you."

The stress from it all must've finally caught up to her, Because Maxine just wilted against me; burying her face into my uninjured shoulder, before her body was wracked with sobs.

I just sighed, holding her weakened body close to me for a moment. I knew the fear would eventually subside . . . much like the way the wound in my shoulder was beginning to heal up; slow and steady, though with several pricks of pain lingering.

The main thing was that she was safe, and alive.

Looking around the room, I winced at the carnage — all the effects of Conner's traps, the bodies of his dead helper and Joanna's still-unconscious form — and knew I had some damage control to work on before I could get Maxine back to the city. Reaching over, I snagged one of the tablecloths off of one of the overturned tables and wrapped it around Maxine's body.

"Stay put, doll . . . I'll be right back," I told her.

Maxine just curled up into a ball, still crying softly.

Rising, I moved to where my coat — singed, but still relatively whole — lay on the floor near the smoking remains of the Molotov bombs. I then moved to where Conner was sprawled out on the floor; trying to crawl away to some hidden door or someplace, one hand clasped to his neck, still whimpering with fear.

I knew he'd survive. Hell, I'd only drawn out barely enough blood to do him any real harm . . . no way was this scumbag gonna get off easy by dying, or even becoming what he most feared. Reaching down, I snagged him by the back of his collar and hauled him upright, onto his feet.

"No, NO!" He went pale as chalk when his eyes focused on me once more.

"Shut up, and listen to me, you asshole!" I

said, snarling as I shoved into his head with my mind; not being too delicate about it, but by then not caring really if I did any further damage to his fragile mental state. "I'm only going to say this once: forget you ever saw me, or my girl, and take your sorry carcass out of this city . . . hell, out of this state, and never come back!"

Nodding feebly, Conner made a strangled reply in his throat.

"Also, don't ever go looking for vampires ever. Understand?" I thrust one finger towards his face for emphasis. "I'm being generous. Any other bloodsucker might not be, get it?"

"y-y-yes!"

I nodded slowly. "Good . . . now, scram!" With that, I shoved him away, watching as he stumbled over his own feet, falling down onto his belly before he scurried off into the shadows like a cockroach; whining this sick, bleating note as he disappeared. Sighing, I shook my head. I hope my reinforcement took. The last thing I needed was him thinking he could come back and cause more trouble!

Turning, I stepped over to where Joanna lay — poor kid! She was still out like a busted light bulb. — and gently turned her over before picking her up to carry her over to Maxine. I had to make sure both of them were okay, though for Joanna's case, I needed to wake her up and perform a little selective 'amnesia' on her. It's not something I like to do but it comes in handy when you don't want some bum remembering he provided me with a little 'snack'.

Reaching for Maxine, I picked her up gently, cradling her shivering form close before I rose up. "Hold on, doll. I'm gonna get you to a doctor," I told her softly.

She didn't say anything to me . . . and yeah, that worried me, but first things first. I had to get her and Joanna back to the blonde's car and then, from there I could worry about taking care of the two dead goons . . . .

Fortunately, halfway back to Vegas, Joanna woke up, finding herself in the backseat of her car — alive, much to her surprise! — with me up front, driving, while Maxine sat huddled in a ball in the passenger seat. It didn't take much to persuade her to take over driving and fortunately she didn't realize the fifteen minutes she lost when I worked through her mind beforehand to remove the memories of this night. The little white lie about her finding me and Maxine on the road, stranded, and in need of help, worked like a charm. Come daybreak, she'd return to her regular routine in the hotel spa, and all it cost me was a real bitch of a headache, having to use my will on her for so long.

I had Joanna drop me and Maxine off just a

few blocks from an all-night clinic. I figured it'd be safer to take her there than a regular hospital; no police to ask too many questions. Even so, I half expected to see some black-and-whites waiting for us when I came through the Emergency Room doors; carrying Maxine in my arms.

Guess Lady Luck was keeping her eyes on Maxine and me, because we didn't run into them or any trouble getting her checked out by the ER docs. It was a pretty slow night, I guess. They were certain she wasn't hurt too badly at first glance, though they did ask her to stick around so one of the OB nurses to do a thorough check.

Maxine and I were left alone in a single, curtained-off corner, with hardly anyone else was there save the techs and nurses at the admission desk. Naturally, the night doctor had me wait outside for the time she took to check Maxine over. I don't think I was more worried about her then, than before when she was in Conner's clutches.

Eventually, the doctor on-call, Doctor Pace, emerged from behind the screen; a rather serious-looking dame, I must admit, with a blond bun and brown eyes behind her wire frame glasses. Taking one last look behind her, she set her eyes on me. "Excuse me, sir?"

I stood up straight. "How is she, Doc?"

"Ms. Reynolds is going to be fine, though she's been through some rough handling and emotional trauma," Dr. Pace said sternly, giving me the evil eye. "You are the one who brought her in, correct?"

"Yes, ma'am," I said evenly.

Her tone was every bit cold as she asked, "Do you know who had done this to her?"

Looks like I wasn't done dodging bullets tonight!

"I assume he's in the hands of the authorities by now, Ma'am. I only just got to her in time to keep any more . . . harm from happening," I said, giving her an iron stare of my own. Geez, I really hoped she didn't push the issue! I didn't need one more brain to clean up and put out on the line tonight!

"I see." Dr. Pace looked down at the clipboard she had been writing notes on. "Well, fortunately there doesn't seem to be any sort of evidence of rape or other sexual misconduct," she said. "At the most, Ms. Reynolds has some abrasions, some bruises and some light head trauma... but, nothing that needs to be looked after overnight."

"Does that mean she's free to go back to her hotel?"

I got another arched look from the doctor for that. "Are you assuming responsibility for her, Mister-?"

"Walker, Ma'am," I said, nodding. "Yes, I'm . . . well, I'm her companion on this visit to Vegas." I stood my ground, knowing full well that if this lady even suspected any misdeeds on my part, she had full right to hold Maxine here until to-morrow. I put on my best 'good-guy' face, add-ing, "I promise, she's in good hands with me, Doc."

She paused, giving me the eye once more... but, I must have convinced her of my good inten-tions, because she said in a less-harsh voice, "I'll have some bed clothes brought in so she can change into something more decent. There are a few pieces of paperwork to finish up, but she should be ready to go in thirty minutes or so."

Sighing, I nodded. "Good. Can I see her now?"

Dr. Pace nodded. "Just be careful, and don't aggravate her further." With that, she pulled the overhead curtain aside, leaning in to speak to Maxine. "Miss, your guardian is here. I'll be back shortly to finish processing your release."

As she walked away, I slowly slipped inside the small space behind the screen, taking a mo-ment to gather myself. There were the signs of the examinations — used surgical gloves in the waste can, a bedside tray filled with instruments and such — and the remains of Maxine's night-dress, folded in a ragged bundle on a nearby stool.

Maxine was perched on a hospital gurney-bed, wearing nothing but one of those blue, back-tie gowns and paper slippers, looking like some lost, lonely bird; her hands folded tightly together in her lap, while she looked down at some distant spot on the tile floor in front of her.

"Hey, Max," I said softly.

She didn't say one word. Sitting there, she looked so different from the woman I remember meeting not so long ago. Drawn in . . . pale and unmoving. Hell, she looked more dead than alive just then.

"Maxine," I said again, "the Doc said you're going to be fine. Just a little bit, and we can blow this pop stand." I tried to smile, but my poor attempt at humor did little to lift even my spirit. Hell! Can't blame her, really. Dropping my gaze to the floor, I stuck my hands in my pockets, not sure what more I could say or do just then. I was so focused on what was going on inside my head, that I almost didn't hear her mumble something.

"Huh? What's wrong?" I asked, looking up at her.

She barely moved her lips. "takemeback."

"Doll?" I started to move towards her, but she flinched like a stung horse, so I backed down.

"Just, take, me, back, to my hotel," she repeated, whispering harshly, never once looking up at me.

I sighed. "Sure, doll. Sure thing."

After Dr. Pace finished all the paperwork, and Maxine was cleaned up and clothed more or less for the better, I got her out to a waiting cab, which whisked us both back up to the 'Rock. Before we left the clinic, Dr. Pace was emphatic that Maxine get straight to bed and get some rest . . . she said she should be okay to return home to New York in a few days, so I made a note to make some changes to her hotel stay and rework her flight reservations.

Heck, I had plenty of cash to fix it so Maxine could stay for as long as she needed . . . provided that she wanted to, after tonight.

Getting back to the hotel, I thanked God that no one was around by the front desk to see me carrying Maxine inside . . . considering there'd been no word about Conner's little fracas on the radio in the cab ride, well, it put me a little at ease that no one was there to ask any questions. Not that they'd get any answers, but still . . . .

Back in her room, I took her straight to the bedroom and put her on the bed — telling her to rest, I'd see to everything else — then, returning to the common area I got on the phone and started making calls. Good thing about Vegas is that, provided you have the cash on hand, people are more than willing to bend over backwards to accommodate your needs. In due time, I had her flight switched to a later one three days from now, and paid up the room's rate until then.

Hanging up the phone, I frowned and sat there on the couch . . . considering my options. The soft gurgle of water, coming through the room walls from the end-suite bathroom got my attention. Rising, I walked back into the bedroom . . . to an empty bed, and a pile of discarded hospital-issue clothes and the remnants of Maxine's lingerie. The door to the bath was partially open, letting some wisps of steam and the lingering fragrance of lemon grass and jasmine waft out into the air.

Getting a nose full of my own aroma . . . phew! A bath didn't sound too bad just then. I smelled like singed, gas-soaked cloth, mixed with my own blood.

Stepping up to the door, I knocked softly. "Doll? You okay in there?"

No reply.

Sighing, I figured I'd better at least look in on her. Opening the door the rest of the way, I slipped inside and leaned against the door frame.

Maxine had forgone the shower, having the wide, oval Jacuzzi tub filled to the max with hot water; which was coated on top with a liberal layer of foamy suds. From one of her bath packets, no doubt. Maxine was sitting in the middle of the tub — hair slicked down wet, her pale face above the clouds of suds — just staring blankly towards the far wall of the bathroom.

Rubbing the back of my head, I sighed and said, "I've got you squared away, both for the room and your flight back East, Maxine. Took a little talking, but I got the manager to see it my way." I gave her a half-smile. "Guess the tip I offered him sorta . . . smoothed things along, I figure."

Maxine didn't say a word. She just kept staring straight ahead.

With a groan, I dropped my chin to my chest, crossing my arms as I asked, "Doll, look, for what it's worth, I didn't have any clue that some screw loose was gonna pull a stunt like tonight. If I'd known-." I cut myself off, just letting the silence fill the steamy air as I stood there, before I said softly, "Maxine, I'm sorry."

"Are you, then."

"Yeah, I am."

There was another span of silence. "That won't cut it, buster."

I looked up at her, seeing her amber eyes fixed on me, practically chilling the air between us. "Doll-."

"Don't you 'Doll' me, Walker," Maxine said, her voice and tone just as sharp as straight-razor steel. "You weren't the one taken at gunpoint and dragged practically naked across an entire city, by some bastard who — as it turns out — was willing to slit my throat, just because I was involved with a bloodsucker."

I blanched, feeling the anger radiating off of her, like waves from a sun lamp. "That bastard threatened to kill me, too, y'know!"

Turning a bit, but keeping her body below the bubbles and suds, Maxine glared at me. "So, that makes it all equal, all around then?" She slapped her hand against the side of the tub, sending a wave of water sloshing over the rim. "Damn it, Walker! You didn't have to play his game like you did; leaving me tied up there while he-!"

"Play?" I asked, forgetting for a moment that I was supposed to keep her calm. "Listen, lady, you think I was having fun, letting that bozo use me for target practice!?" I turned and threw a fist out, smashing my knuckles against the tile wall. "Ow! Damn it!" I rubbed my fist, scowling at the cracked tile. "This was not what I had in mind to deal with tonight."

Turning her head away, Maxine said sourly, "It wasn't what I had planned, that's for certain."

I grunted. "Hell, next time I'll make sure to work my next rumble with a wanna-be killer around your schedule."

"That wasn't funny!" Maxine hissed, "Do you think this is a big joke?"

I turned back and scowled. "Do you see me laughing, Doll?"

She nearly burst out from the tub at that crack. "Don't you call me that, you . . . you-!"

"What?" I asked, glaring down at her, even as a part of me was practically beating at the side of my head to calm down. "What were you going to say, Max?" I tried to keep my temper in check, though, when I caught a glance at myself in the bathroom mirror just then, I could see my eyes were burning with an indigo haze and the tips of my fangs were protruding just past the edge of my lips.

Hell, just what I didn't need! Clamping down on my emotions, I forced myself down from the slow burn building up in my chest and head.

Maxine, for her part, must've clued in to how close I was to letting go of my 'beast' again. She sank back down into the water, appearing to huddle against the far side of the tub. "I don't know . . . just don't say anything to me!"

Letting out a deep sigh, I started to move towards her, putting a hand out in a calming motion. "Look, Max-."

"Don't!"

It was only one word, but from the way she suddenly flattened herself against the porcelain and tile wall, her arm out in a shielding motion towards me, it had all the impact of a forty-five to my chest. I stopped moving, taking in the wide-eyed, fearful expression on her face. I didn't want this. Her fear, her distrust . . . it was all there, naked as she was, open for me to see in all its ugly, stark appearance.

I let my hand drop. "Okay . . . fine. It's okay. I won't-." I bit my lip. "I'd never-."

"Just get out of here, Walker," Maxine said, soft yet hard as ice again. "Get out. Leave me alone."

Sighing, I nodded. "Whatever you say, doll." I said, closing my eyes for a moment as I turned towards the bathroom doorway. Stepping out into the bedroom beyond, I grasped the door handle and pulled the white-panel door shut behind me. Hell.

I slouched against the wall next to the bathroom door; rubbing my temples as I tried to think past the ice and pain inside me. Not that I had any reason to deny that I didn't deserve to feel this lousy. After all, if it hadn't been for this . . . 'condition' I was in, perhaps then Maxine wouldn't have been threatened, roughed up and all, right?

Still, I can't lay all of this on my being a vampire. That crutch won't hold much weight. Truth is, I knew something like this was bound to happen; sooner or later.

Pushing myself off the wall, I moved towards the bed and sat down, sighing through my teeth while I listened to the faint sounds of water splashing inside the closed bathroom. One thing I did know, because of everything, Maxine had finally seen my blacker side; the 'beast', as it were. I can't erase the memory of the look on her face — scared, for herself — and, I just knew hanging around her from now on . . . that feeling wasn't going to go away.

So, what to do? I asked myself.

Facing the cold facts, such as they were to

me, there really was only one thing to do . . . .

It didn't take me long. I was used to packing up everything I had in a moment's notice, considering what I dealt with being what I am. I often wonder what some of the so-called experts on vampires would say, given the fact I'm practically a transient bloodsucker, hm?

I had everything stuffed in the two duffels — practically everything I own or hold dear to me — and waiting by the door of Maxine's room, before I made one last check to see if I'd missed anything. I ended up leaving a few things we'd collected in the span of our short time together; a couple of token things, pictures and stuff she'd gotten from a few of the Vegas attractions.

There was this one picture I found . . . thought about keeping it, since it was something taken off the cuff by a savvy photographer over by one of the ritzy hotels. It had me and Maxine, locked in a embrace while we were dancing, right in front of those musical fountains they have on display; both of us smiling like we'd had no cares in all the wide world.

Like I said . . . I thought about keeping it. Ended up leaving it on the dresser, along with everything else I didn't want to take away from her. I mean, why not leave her with some sort of happy reminder, right?

Though I had this feeling it might end up in the garbage, after tonight.

In any case, I left the bedroom and headed for the door. Yeah, I should've gone and told Maxine I was leaving. Yet, she made it clear she didn't want to see me, so . . . I've always been a guy never to refuse a woman's wishes, after all.

I really didn't pay attention when I made my way down to the lobby, considering how numb I was feeling about then. It wasn't until I was outside of the lobby's main entrance, that I got myself back together in time to notice a rainstorm had moved in while I'd been seeing to Maxine. In fact, the first cool drops were just starting to fall, when I stepped up to the curbside valet station, making me shrug deeper into my battered overcoat.

A young fellow manning the station turned and asked me, "Call for your car, Sir?"

I just shook my head. "Don't have one, kid. Get me a cab, though?"

"Right away!" He turned and picked up the call phone, talking briskly into it for a moment.

Looking away, I jammed my hands into my pockets . . . and felt something flat and thin in the left one.

Frowning, I pulled it out, staring at the square of white plastic, with the 'Rock's logo printed across the front of it, and a strip of black down the one side . . . ah, Maxine's room key. Must've forgot about it in all the hullabaloo tonight. I started to turn to the valet to give it to him-.

"Sir, I'll be right with you," he said, turning briefly to smile at me before he scribbled something on a clipboard. "Cab's coming up in a minute." Turning away, he motioned towards the front lobby, calling for another staff member to come out.

Can't really explain it — maybe I never will know myself — but when he started talking to the other guy that ran up, I just stuck the room key back into my pocket. Guess maybe I just wanted something to remind me of the past few days. Not that I needed one, really . . . as a vampire, you sort of get this other ability: a long memory and almost perfect recall.

Yeah, this time in Vegas was going to stick with me for a long, long time. Damnit. Sometimes, being what I am can be a hell of a curse.

It was just about then that a Yellow Cab hack arrived at the curbside. The valet and his fellow staffer moved to open the nearside door and put my two bags into the trunk. I shrugged, stepping over to get inside, ducking into the open doorway as the kid turned and said, "Thanks for staying with us, sir. We look forward to you again real soon."

I just nodded. "Sure, kid. Thanks." I passed him a twenty, before pulling myself inside the backseat compartment, letting him close the door tight behind me.

Inside, the driver — a dark-haired guy with a Latino's complexion — turned and asked, "Where do you want to go?"

I leaned back in the seat and sighed. "How about Chicago?"

That earned me a laugh. "Only if you got ten-grand, plus gas money I'll need it for th' round trip, man!"

I sighed softly. "Not tonight, friend . . . how about, the Dew Drop Inn?"

The guy glanced at the 'Rock, then back at me, before shrugging and turning around to put the hack in gear. "Sure thing," he said, slapping the duty-switch on his meter. "Hold on tight." With that, he stepped on the gas, and we pulled away from the hotel and merged into the late-night traffic.

I let myself slouch down in the back seat. Brother, I felt tired . . . down to the bone and marrow-kind of tired. Well, so much for trying to pick up my spirits. What had started out as an adventure, was now sliding back down towards that grim, gray valley I'd fallen into before I got to this town. Well, for what it's worth . . . I can't say I didn't enjoy the time, while we were together.

Turning back around to face the front of the hack, I closed my eyes and muttered to the driver, "Just wake me when we get there, Mac."

"Sure, man . . . will do."

With that, I said a silent word, directed back to that red-headed dame, now lost to me: *Take care, Max. If we're lucky, we won't see each other, not ever again.*

STEPHEN R. SOBOTKA

TWO OF A KIND

6. - Get An After-Life.

I'm standing in the middle of the desert
Waiting for my ship to come in
But now no joker, no jack, no king
Can take this loser hand and make it win . . . .

— "Leaving Las Vegas", Sheryl Crow

TWO OF A KIND

I had every intention of just shacking up and sleeping off through the day, then — when I could get to a phone the following night — call the airlines, get a one-way ticket back to my home turf.

My thoughts were once I was back home, I'd hopefully forget about the disastrous turn this little pick-me-up trip had taken and . . . well, never hear about anything remotely related to the Strip ever, ever again. Not Conner. Not even Joanna or even . . . Max?

Hell.

I'd been taught by some of the best cardsharks and players in the game, when to realize when you're sitting there at the table with a busted hand and what to do about it. Always trust the rules, son; take what you've got, get up and leave and never look back. Once you look back, you're doomed to just finish the hand you've been dealt, and then you have to take the consequences that go with it.

I knew I had to step away. I knew I had to get up and go, and yet . . . there was one thing.

Maxine.

Hell.

So, here I am. Still in Vegas.

Actually, I'm back in the place that started this whole roller coaster ride; Frankie's Bar.

It's been two days since the night I had to leave the girl who . . . hell, I should just admit it. She was the one woman that had come along in a long, long time, who made me feel more alive than I'd felt in ages. Yet, thanks to the part of me she'd once said 'didn't matter', she now thought I was worse that the scum that had tried to kill her.

So, here I am; sitting back at the same spot on the end of the bar, on the same seat, with the same kind of drink sitting beside me. Yet, for all the oblivion that the alcohol promised to give me, I had yet to take one sip. Instead, I was cracking peanuts and flicking the shells into an empty bowl a few feet down the bar.

"Hey, Buddy!"

I sighed, looking up at the familiar sight of Joey, who was in the process of slipping away from a couple drinking some flowery concoctions at the other end of the bar. "Yeah?"

"Listen, I don't mean to seem like I'm pryin', but . . . what in all that's holy are you doin' here?" His faded vest looked a little more worn than usual as it folded away from his sizable gut, and his hair looked a little thinner up top . . . but, maybe it was because Maxine had been sweet on him, back when we first met, that I didn't tell him to take a hike.

"I mean," he said, ducking his head a little to look into my eyes as he slouched over the bar top. "I thought you an' Maxine had, well . . . you know?"

I sighed thickly, dropping my face from view again. Yeah, I knew.

I trapped an empty peanut shell between to fingers, letting it rest there before turning it around so that I had the point of my index finger behind it. "It's not anything worth talkin' about," I muttered, giving the shell a savage flick. It caromed off of a beer glass halfway down the bar, rocketing into the air before striking the surface of the mirror behind Joey. "Just drop it."

"Drop it? Drop it!" The surprise in Joey's voice matched the rising pitch level for level. "You've gotten the favor of a dame that's the envy of every whale, high-roller and card-jockey from the Luxor to Caesar's, and right now you're not with her? Chum, in case you've been livin' underground for the past few years, I'm gonna clue you in to a few things about Maxine."

I scowled, "Listen, pal-."

Joey barged ahead, cutting me off at the pass. "Maxine is probably one of the nicest dames I've ever had the honor of servin' drinks to, in all the years I've been workin' the Strip. She's a dish that can't be compared to. I mean, you could have breakfast, lunch and dinner outta her, and still have enough for a nice dessert later!"

I nearly had to laugh at that. "Yeah . . . you are, so right on that score, chum." Turning the glass between my fingers, I nodded and half cocked my head to the side.

Joey went on, looking at me more soberly, "In all the years I've seen her come to Vegas, she's never so much as given any of the mooks that come through those doors the invitation she gave you!" Wiping off the bar top, he added, "One thing about her . . . she loves to party, but it's a rare thing when she brings a fella back to her place. Capish?"

I had to agree with him there. She as much as admitted that to me, even before we'd gotten back to her place our first night together.

"So, somethin' must've come up between you two," Joey said. "Otherwise, I really doubt you'd be getting drunk in my bar, or am I not right about this?"

"I still wish I could tell you what's wrong, Joe." I sighed, staring at the red-concoction filling my untouched glass. "I really wish I could." I leaned back in my barstool and continued to stare at my drink, and Joey seemed to take the hint . . . that or someone down the bar had motioned to him for another drink.

Either way, he slouched off and left me to stew in my own inner turmoil.

It couldn't have been much longer after that — minutes, an hour, who knew, really. — when someone came up to the bar as Joey finished pulling a few mugs of beer for a customer.

"*Excuse me . . . can you tell me, if there's a John Walker here?*"

That broke through my dark mood, real quick!

Turning, I spied a young fellow, dressed in the casual shirt and outfit of the 'Rock Hotel's shuttle service, standing in front of Joey with a small clipboard in his hand. Before I could move or say anything, Joey pointed a thumb in my direction and asked the kid something in reply. There was a small exchange, with the young fellow making several gestures towards the clipboard, while Joey gave him some sharper gestures, and most likely some equally cutting words to boot, before the kid finally pulled something off the clipboard and handed it over to him.

Joey dug out some bills from his vest pocket and gave them over, nodding as the young man headed to the exit. He then turned towards me — holding what looked like a folded piece of paper in his hand — and moved down along the bar; his face filled with a dark look.

That should've set off some red flags in my head, right then and there.

"Got somethin' for you, Bud . . . from our girl," Joey said, his tone sharp.

I sat up a bit. "Max?" Looking at the paper for a second, I asked, "What's-?"

"That fella was told to deliver this to you, on the proviso you could be found. Considering he's been to nearly every dive and roach-motel off the Strip, I gotta give him kudos for just bein' able to find you in this place," Joey said, cutting me off as he gave me the old hairy-eyeball. " Now, I gotta wonder . . . just what did you do to Maxine that was so bad, that she had to send someone else practically all over the city, just to deliver a message!?" He held up the paper between two fingers and scowled at me.

Scowling back, I didn't let my temper get the better of me. I mean, he was only protecting her, right? "That's between me and her, Joe."

Joey didn't budge. "Ah-huh, and that makes it all nice-nice with everyone concerned, hm? To me, it don't look so good for you, chum."

I looked at him squarely. "Are you gonna give that to me, or just keep tearin' strips out of me all night?"

Joey stared at me for a moment longer, before he put the paper down on the bar top and snorted. "I wager there's worse that she could do to ya, chum," he said, before moving off to start cleaning glasses nearby.

Sighing, I reached out and pulled the paper towards me, before picking it up. Looking at it briefly, while letting my senses linger over it as well. There wasn't a trace of Maxine's scent on this; just the clean, neutral smell of processed paper and the slight chemical touch of ink. Opening the paper, I looked past the bright, hotel logo and found a neat, paragraph of text below:

Bud, My flight back to NYC leaves tomorrow, but I need to give you something. Come to my room, before sunrise.

- Maxine

Funny thing, it didn't read like she was being playful, or spiteful or any sort of 'ful'-feeling I could name. I read the note over and over again . . . and, for the life of me I couldn't tell just what this game was about. If that's what it was. A part of me started tugging at my sense of self-preservation; drop it, get out of town and don't look back.

Smart advice, really . . . yet, there was another part of me that was nudging me towards doing just what the note said: go and see her. May be the last time, but you owe her a better goodbye than just a written one left on a hotel dresser.

Clenching my hand, I made the note crinkle as I crushed the paper up. Damn . . . what was a body to do? It could be just that, just a chance to say 'hey, thanks for the good time, while they lasted.' . . . .

Talk about torn between two primal forces! Saving my own skin or making closure. It wasn't a choice I thought I'd have to make when I got up tonight.

From where he was making himself busy, Joey looked at the crumpled note in my hand. "Bad news?"

"Problems, Joe. Just, problems and . . . more so." I dropped off into silence, my eyes still fixed on my glass, watching the celery stalk sink slowly into the melting, crimson sludge.

Joey paused in cleaning a mug for a second, then shook his head. "Well, whatever it is, I don't think it's your fault, chum."

I almost had to laugh harshly at the sarcasm in his tone! *Not my fault!* Oh sure! Not my fault some whacko jerk fingered me for a vampire. Not my fault he followed me and Maxine around, before kidnapping her to use as bait for a trap to kill me . . . with the promise of killing her as well.

"Yeah, sure," I muttered softly, balling up the note before I tossed it away from me; watching as it skipped down the bar top before coming to rest against an empty pretzel bowl.

Joey frowned, pausing to swipe the bowl and the wadded note with one hand. "Sheesh. People just can't seem to get through this life without making a mess or two 'round this place!"

Of course, there just had to be a double-meaning there, right kids?

Truth was, I did make a mess of things . . . so, what was I going to do about it?

"Ah, hell!" I muttered, shifting on my seat to get to my wallet. "How much I owe you, Joe?"

Joey looked up, then down at my unfinished drink. "What's your hurry, Buster?" he asked, arching one eyebrow as I got up on my feet.

"Somethin' I gotta do," I replied, fishing out a ten-spot to slap it on the counter. "Keep the change, 'kay?" I snagged my overcoat from where I draped it on the back of the barstool and started walking towards the exit.

I should have gone right back to Maxine's motel . . . but, I still had to fight with myself as I walked back along the strip. It wasn't the best of nights to walk, what with another rainstorm overhead. I could just see the looks of the people passing by in their hacks and cars... as well as those rushing to get inside the casinos and attractions.

Must've looked like a loony bird, with my hat and overcoat slicked down with the wet. Still, walking has always been a means for me to get myself grounded. There's just something about putting your feet on solid ground, feeling every foot of distance between where you've been and where you're going to.

Yeah, deep stuff I know. Sue me for being that kind of a person sometimes.

Eventually, I made it back to the hotel. I stalked past the lobby, the slots in front of the casino-proper and grabbed the closest elevator; getting one odd look from the concierge, and just lucky that the cab didn't stop until it reached her floor and walked the last few yards to her doorway.

I paused on the carpeted hallway outside of Maxine's room, looking down at the electronic lock and it's sole, red light glowing steadily in the faceplate. I lifted one hand to knock . . . and stopped it just an inch above the door, before I let it drop back to my side. Knocking just . . . well, it didn't feel right!

I stuck my hand into my pocket . . . and found the edge of the old keycard that I'd kept, before snagging it and pulling it out into view. Well, it might still work. I reasoned, flipping the small, plastic rectangle over and over in my hand. Then again . . . Maxine surely would've asked them to change her room access over, after she discovered I'd was gone, right?

Standing there, I could hear my mind wrestling with both heart and logic: *Geez, what are you doing, pal? Stop being like an odd-ball and just go in. She'd invited you back, so what was there to worry about?*

Plenty, the paranoid part of my braincase was screaming. *She said she had 'something to give me'. What if that turned out to be a quick death with a burning stake? She could have appropriated one of the hotel's fire axes to chop my head off?*

Of course, a hot stake's better than a cold chop any day.

Groaning, I turned and started to walk away . . . only to get about three steps down the hall, before I whipped back around and glared at that damn locked door again. *C'mon, John! Get a hold of yourself. Getting paranoid isn't going to help you out. Not this time.*

I clenched my hand around the edges of the key card, feeling myself go all iron inside. I took one step, then one more . . . turning towards the doorway, squaring my shoulders like I was about to jump into a roughneck bar in the Southside of town.

"Okay . . . just go by the numbers," I muttered.

Lifting my hand, I flipped the card over and jammed it into the slot on the door lock. There was a muted *click!*, and the red light turned green.

Hell, roll me on green felt and call me lucky.

Yanking the card out, I gripped the handle and twisted, pushing the door open wide. Stepping inside, I could see the room beyond had been dimmed, with all but one of the lamps on the side table lit.

Well, she wasn't waiting just inside the doorway, ready to leap out like some wailing banshee. So far, so good, right? Still a bit on edge, I slowly made my way across the carpeted floor. I called out softly, "Max? Maxine?"

"I'm here, John Walker . . . in the bedroom." The reply came softly from behind the shut door on the other side of the common room.

Perfect. Shuffling over to the closed door, I could still feel a part of me screaming for me to turn around and get out. Get out, while I still had breath and the means to do so. Yet, if fate is waiting in there . . . hell! Best not to keep the lady waiting, right?

I took a deep breath and stepped up to the bedroom door and slowly opened it. The first thing that hit me was the smell. Not a sick, bitter smell of fear or something else unmentionable, but the delicate aroma of scented paraffin; vanilla, cinnamon and . . . jasmine, a scent I'd never forget.

Opening the door further, I got a view of the far side of the room; the curtains drawn closed over the wide window, while the overhead light was dimmed to a soft level of illumination. I took a quick look around, spying several lighted candles spread across the dresser near the doorway; the source of the relaxing scents in the air.

That made me lower my guard a bit. I mean, if this was still a trap of some kind . . . it was the oddest one I'd ever come up against, let me tell you.

Turning away from the door, I looked into the center of the room and there she was; clothed in a simple, short sleeved blue dress with a gently pleated skirt that hung a inch or so below her knees, with a pair of matching shoes on her feet.

"Hi," she offered softly, with a fragile smile that hit me like a slow sip of double-malt whiskey; warm as sweet as it set a fire down the middle of me.

"Hi, yourself," I replied thickly, looking at her face like I wanted to recommit it to my memory; seeing her red hair and amber eyes, accented with just a touch of eye shadow, and her lips covered with a fine sheen of gloss. Gods . . . I never did forget how good she looked, even though seeing her again was like like it was all brand new to me, again.

"I'm . . . I'm really glad, you made it here," she said, a slight flush of color rising in her cheeks, clearly reacting from the open admiration in my eyes.

"Well, I, ah . . . can't say that I'm . . . not sad to be here," I said, still a bit unsure as to what was on her agenda, even though looking at her just then did put a good number of my fears to rest. "You . . . ah, said you-?"

"John," she said, looking at me with those amber eyes glittering in the candlelight, "don't talk." Lifting one slim hand, her index finger crooked towards herself. "C'mere."

Stepping closer, I tried to keep my cool. Wasn't easy, considering the state of my emotions just then. She looked up at me, before raising her hands to unfasten the front of my overcoat; lingering briefly on some spots that bore scorch marks from the night before. I didn't say a word as she reaching up with both hands to open my coat and push it off my shoulders, before she nodded towards my head. I removed my hat and tossed it towards a chair in the corner.

"Sit," Maxine said simply, motioning towards the edge of the bed.

Following her lead, I did ask she asked. Sitting down next to me, keeping a foot of space between us, she dropped her gaze from mine, fixing her eyes on one spot on my chest, before she inhaled deeply. "I have to get this out . . . so, bear with me, okay?

"John, the other night . . . what I said before when I, well . . . I know now it was just my reaction to everything that's happened-."

"Max," I offered gently, "you don't have to say-."

"No, I do. Please just . . . let me finish, okay?"

I held my tongue, and just nodded.

"Ever since you left, I've been thinking . . . and, I realize what happened wasn't your fault. After all, you didn't ask that jerk to come after us, and you did save me from him, for which, I am grateful. Still, you have to know, after what happened . . . I wasn't sure that I wanted to see you ever again." She looked down at her hands. "I mean, if that was the sort of thing that happens on a regular basis . . .?"

This was getting into troubled waters here! I reached up to cover her hands with my own. "Hey, I'll admit, it's been nearly ten years since the last dope tried to make me do a Lagossi-death scene," I half-joked. I could feel the tension in her hands. *Brother, she was working through some major stuff here! Don't drag it out*. I told myself. "But . . . I'll be frank. I honestly don't go looking for trouble, Maxine. It just, well, seems to find me sometimes."

Nodding her head, Maxine replied with a short laugh, "Yeah, well, I can understand why."

I couldn't help the lop-sided grin that filled

my face. "I'm from Chicago, doll . . . what can I say?" We both laughed at that, but . . . when the laughter died off, silence filled the room; so thick, I thought it would smother the mood.

"Believe me, I know what you're thinking right now . . . what you might be expecting and . . . I mean, any other girl would have just dropped you like a hot brick, before saying, 'Thanks for the fun, but I can't handle the weirdoes, Bye!'."

I had to work a knot out of my throat. *Ooo, brother. Here it comes.* I thought.

"Still, with everything that has happened, there's just two things that need to be said."

That got me off-center for a bit. "Oh? What's that?"

"One, that I'm not like any other girl." That's when she shook her head twice, before looking back up at me; those amber eyes glittering. "Two, I- . . . I'm in love with you, John."

Ladies, you ever want to knock a guy's entire life off its axis, just tell him those words.

"You . . . what?" I asked, unsure if I dared to believe her.

"I, love, you, John Walker." That's when she slid across the gap between us, pressed herself against me as she flung her arms around me in a fierce hug! Burying her face in my chest, she hugged me so tight I thought she was gonna pop some ribs loose!

"Oof!" As gently as I could, I put my arms

around her, while a million questions whipped by my brain.

Truth be told, I couldn't answer a single, blessed one of them, nor did I care to even try. All that mattered to me just then, just now, was the fact that Maxine was there . . . and she said she loves me! Even as off-kilter as I was, I couldn't help the feeling that burst out of me; shattering the ball of ice that had frozen my guts. I literally felt myself melting as I dropped my head so my cheek was pressed against her red hair.

Yeah, I'd only known this gal . . . of what, a few days now? Still . . . I couldn't deny how she made me feel, and how I felt about her.

I slowly let out the breath I'd been holding. "Maxine . . . I," I murmured, stopping only briefly to clear my throat from the tightness that threatened to render me mute. "I . . . I love you too, doll."

Maxine wrapped her arms around me tighter, before she pulled back to look up at me again. "Then . . . I guess, there's just one last thing." Before I could utter one word, she moved to press a finger to my lips, before giving me a soft smile. With a small shudder, Maxine slowly closed her eyes . . . and turned her head to the right, tilting it back so that the long side of her neck was presented to me.

"D-Doll?"

"Please?" Her reply was barely a whisper, no

more than a soft kiss from an ethereal angel. She pulled me closer, making no mistake to her intent . . . what she was asking me to do!

My head filled with all kinds of sensory input: her scent, the rapid, expectant beating pulse of her heart, the heat under the surface of her skin. Oh, the 'beast' in me was practically roaring: *take her! She wants you to do it! Take her now!*

Believe me, brother, I was more than ready to do just that... but, reaching up, I put my fingertips against her right cheek and slowly turned her head back around to face mine.

"John?" Her eyes opened up wide in surprise.

"I understand, but . . . that's not what I want," I said softly. Ducking my head, I stopped the question about to fly from her lips with my own, slipping my hand over her cheek to keep her from pulling away. I didn't so much as ravish her mouth. Instead, I kept it firm but gentle, sweet yet hot. The way they say that 'The Kiss' is supposed to be like.

For a bit, Maxine tried to stop it, but then, she was kissing me back with equal love. Her hands slid over my shoulders and up into my hair; long nails curling through my dark locks like she was clinging to a lifeline.

Eventually, we broke off and gazed at one another. She said one word: "Lily?"

"Yeah."

"Ah," Maxine closed her eyes, this time in

acceptance.

Even with all the blood thundering in my ears — raw lust vibrating through every fiber and bone — I stood up slowly and gently pulled Maxine up to join me. Running my fingertips along her arms, I moved them towards the buttons at the front of her dress . . . and, pausing just to get the nod of permission from her, I started undoing them one at at time. As the front of her dress parted slowly, Maxine reached up and undid the buttons at the cuffs of my shirt, before she mirrored my movements; exposing my bare chest at the same time as I peeled the two halves of her dress back.

"Geez," I said softly, taking in the cream hued demi-bra and panty set she wore. A pair of thigh-high stockings — topped with simple lace stays — helped to draw attention to her lower body and the damp patch of her crotch.

With a small smile, Maxine said, "See what you do to me . . . Bud?" I couldn't reply, but that didn't stop her from moving my opened shirt off my shoulders. Eventually, she pressed in close again, and I could feel the silken touch of her skin against my own as we embraced. Then, I felt the soft touch of her lips as she kissed her way across my chest.

Mercy! How could she do something so simple, and have it make me feel like a river of sparks going through me?

Sighing, I tugged her dress off of her shoulders, letting it slip to the floor in a puddle of fabric, before I tucked the heel of my left shoe beneath my right to slip it off, following suit with the other. Seeing what I was doing, Maxine kicked off her own shoes and nudged them aside, before she let her hands drift over my naked skin.

"Mm . . . you're shivering," she said.

I was. "Can't help it."

"Let me make you warm." Letting her hands drift low around my waist, she pulled me closer and stretched up to trail more kisses along my jaw, reaching for my lips. So engaged as we were above, her hands moved below to find my belt . . . unbuckling and undoing the buttons on my fly. A soft clink heralded the landing of my trousers on the floor.

With a low growl, I slowly parted from our lip lock, before turning Maxine around and pulling her close to me. Reaching up, I found the bra's clasp between her shoulders, unfastening it with a soft snap before I slipped my hands under the straps to push them over her shoulders. As it fell away, I smiled as I looked down to view her breasts . . . just as soft and delicious as I remembered!

"Oh!" Ramona gasped as my hands cupped each orb, with her nipples turning to stone-tips against the surface of my palms. Arching, she pressed her chest into them while her bottom squirmed against my front. "Mmm . . . yes," she hissed.

Rolling each nipple, I bent down to nuzzle her ear. "Mm, hell . . . I'm sorry I was such a jerk," I whispered.

"Well, you were a jerk . . . but, you can make it up to me." Maxine moaned, before she turned and placed a light smooch on my neck.

"Mmm, I think I have an idea on that," I said, chuckling as I nudged her towards the bed; making her fall onto the comforter before bouncing to rest against the pillows.

Turning halfway to look at me, Maxine's eyes flashed as she saw me bend down to strip off my socks and step out of my rumpled pants. "Oh, do you?" she said, her voice thick as she watched me move onto the mattress. She leaned back to meet me halfway, her arm slipping around my neck as she welcomed me with a steamy kiss. Together, we wrapped each other up in a tumble of limbs and caressing hands; touching every exposed inch of skin, savoring our own warmth and closeness. Kisses were followed by nibbles, licks and nips to sensitive areas, fanning our passions to a warmth that became unbearable to hold back.

It was while I was dipping low to drill my tongue into her navel, that Maxine — running one hand through my dark locks — sighed and murmured, "John . . . please, don't-AH! Don't . . . I can't wait, I . . . I want you!"

Looking up from between her legs, I smiled

and lifted up . . . from the stiffness beneath me, I clearly didn't want to wait any more either. "Always give a lady . . . what she wants," I panted. The scent of both of our aroused bodies was filling the air around us, filling my senses with an erotic fog. Reaching up, I hooked my fingers under the sides of her panties and tugged them down. Wriggling, Max helped me out by lifting up, letting me get them down and off of her gams, before she spread her thighs wide for me.

Running my hands up her stocking-clad legs, I moved in closer, chuckling hoarsely when I felt her lift her knees up and place her feet against the sides of my boxers.

"Oops," I said, watching as she worked them down my hips with her toes.

"Forgot something . . . Bud?" she asked, her smile a lusty smirk as she felt me lean up, while reaching down with one hand to help her get my underwear clear of my throbbing dick.

"Nah," I said, lowering myself until I was braced on both my knees and elbows over her. "I've got . . . everything well in hand."

"Actually," she murmured, her eyes dropping into half-closed, smoky, amber slits as she reached down to position me at her pussy, "I think, I have everything-OOH!" Her words drew up into a sharp gasp, as the moment she'd seated the cap of my prick between her folds, I thrust into her with a single, slow thrust. "Ah-mmm . . . Bud!"

she crooned.

With a deep sigh of satisfaction, I smiled as I lowered myself down to cover her body. "Thanks, doll . . . just enjoy," I said warmly. Closing my eyes, I savored the wet-silk feel of her inner walls, clutching at my solid flesh as I remained still for a heartbeat or two. *Geez, I could've let this woman go . . . and never known-!* Shoving that thought aside, I slowly started to pull back, then push forward into the wet Universe of flesh connecting us.

Wrapping her arms over my shoulders, Maxine purred against my neck and ear as she let me work between her legs. Before too long, she lifted her legs and clamped them around my thrusting hips; rising up to match me, move for move, as the sparks pooling at our joined sexes began to form into flames of increasing magnitude.

"Ohh, geezus . . . Max," I whispered, my breath hot against the shell of her ear as I let myself shift up a gear; my pelvis slapping against hers with a smack-smack-smack of moist flesh. Sweat was collecting on our bodies, mixing with the flavors of our aroused scents. God! Was there nothing better, I ask you?

Moaning and shaking, Max was twisting her hips, trying to keep as much contact between our bodies as this turned into a rolling, rutting fuck between us. "Mm, ah . . . AH, damn it, Bud!"

Clutching at my back, she was making harder for me to move inside her, but the friction between her puss and my dick made the fires grow and grow, no matter how limited my range of motion was.

I swear, I wanted to have this last for a lifetime . . . until the whole place came crashing down in flames around us. All too soon, I could feel the tell-tale signs of her climax approaching fast; her honey-sweet walls grasping tighter to my cock-flesh, while her breathing and moans turned to pants and high-pitched wails. Our bodies rubbing together like matches, I knew we weren't going to survive the conflagration to come . . . when either of us came first!

"Ah! Ah, ah-huh . . . AH! John!" Maxine's voice shot up a notch, as her muscles locked me tight against her body.

Feeling my own trigger about to trip, I buried my face into her red-gold hair and groaned as the waves of pleasure started racing down my spine. "Hmmm . . . doll, ahh! AH!" Before I could do anything more, I felt a jerk as Max's body went still, then she began to shake as the first shocks of her orgasm hit . . . and hit hard!

"Oh GOD!" Maxine cried out; her voice strained as she wailed through wave after wave of her release.

That did it for me; unable to cope I climaxed and fell onto her with a grunt as I felt myself spend deep into her pussy. "Geez-zus-AAH!"

The last time we'd made love . . . hell, it was nothing compared to this! I thought I'd shattered down to the bone, and turned to mush as I emptied myself into her; all body and soul gone in one supreme climb to the sumit of passion.

Eventually, our bodies stopped rocking in the aftershocks of our mutual orgasm. I felt completely drained . . . not just from below, but literally every part of my body felt ready to fall into a coma! Moving to roll over onto my side, I kept Max tucked in close to my body as I sank into the mattress. She moaned softly, her arms and legs wrapped around me as we cradled each other . . . and, somehow — though I can't remember who did it — we ended up under the sheets, our heads resting on the pillows.

The last memory I had, was the scent of her hair in my nose, just before my brain went fugue.

When I could think straight again, I found myself with a drying film of sweat over me, under the rumpled sheets of Maxine's large bed as I came out of a restful sleep.

Oh yeah, Maxine was there too.

Lifting up, I looked down at her; spooned up against me with my right arm wrapped around her from behind, resting between her breasts. She was still dozing, equally sweaty and mussed up from our session of lovemaking . . . and looking better than any of those pinup girls I'd seen over the years of my inhuman existence.

I could have woken her to share in that sweet euphoria I was savoring... but, nah! She looked peaceful - more so then than she had been following our run in with Conner - so, I just let her snooze while I held her close.

Eventually, she did blink her eyes and slowly came out of her sleep. With a great, heaving sigh that sounded full of satisfaction, she smiled and said, "'Lo."

"Hello yourself, doll," I replied, giving her a soft squeeze. "You okay?"

Nodding, Maxine turned around and pressed herself against me, wrapping her arms around my neck to lever herself higher up on the bed. "Yeah, I'm more than okay. Yet-."

"What?" I asked.

Lifting her face from where it was nuzzled against my chest, Maxine fixed her eyes onto mine. "I remember what Lily had done to you . . . but, was that the only reason why didn't you do it, Bud?"

"Do it?"

She tilted her head sideways, exposing the spot on her neck where I'd bitten her the first time. The spots had all but healed. In fact, all that I could see just then were two small puckers of raised flesh, which would soon vanish when they healed completely.

Okay, so I was a bit slow just then. You try to function on all gears after someone gives you the screwing of a lifetime, and see how well you do.

Looking back at me, she pressed on with, "You didn't take me. I just don't understand. Aren't vampires-?"

I pressed a finger to her mouth. "Max, you've been listening to the wrong people! Just because we made love, and how I feel about you, doesn't mean I *have* to turn you into what I am."

"But," she asked, "Didn't Lily-?"

I shook my head slowly. "Lily had been turned when she was still a young kid, far as I know." I got thoughtful for a moment. "Come to think of it now, I'm pretty sure she turned me because she didn't think we could survive any other way." I looked at Maxine squarely. "But, I couldn't turn the woman I love into a vampire, too."

Maxine blinked, tightening her grip on me. "Still, wouldn't be, y'know . . . easier if-?"

I rose up to prop myself on my elbow, looking down at her wide-eyed expression. Funny, to see her look so surprised. "To be perfectly honest, I'd rather you stay just the way you are; normal, human and without a sudden need for maximum sunscreen."

That got a soft giggle out of her. "But, what happens to us now? How do we stay together?"

"Doll, how does anyone stay together these days?" I asked, a small smile on my kisser. "Max, after what we just did, do you even have to ask how I feel about you?" She shook her head. "So, we hold onto what we've have for each other, and work out the details from there. Besides . . . you've got to return to New York, right?"

Rising up to sit next to me, Maxine let her hands drift over my chest slowly. "That's true . . . but-?"

"So, you don't neglect your responsibilities, neither do I . . . and in the meantime, you get a little incentive," I prompted. Making a decision, I looked down at the floor next to the bed, where I found my pants crumpled up in a pile.

"Incentive?" Max asked.

"Incentive." I quickly leaned over, feeling around inside the pockets for a moment, before returning to her side. "Here," I said, handing her the brass key I'd fished out.

Taking it, she looked at me oddly. "What's this?"

"One of the master keys to my apartment, back in Chicago," I explained. "

"But, why give me this?"

"Like I said, it's some incentive. You can come to visit me in Chicago, any time you want, and no matter if I'm asleep during the day or out for a bit, that key will let you in. Just let me know ahead to time, I'll have everything ready and waiting for you."

Maxine wrapped her hand around the key, closing her eyes before she smiled in a sort of dreamy-like manner. "You mean that?"

I had to grin before I asked, "As long as I'm invited to drop in on you in the Big Apple in return?"

At that, Maxine slid up over me, looking down at me with a crooked smile. "Hmmm, I dunno... isn't it a written that one never invites a vampire into her house?"

I wrapped one arm around her waist, letting a flicker of power flash across my eyes, making them glow. "Consider the alternative; not inviting a particular vampire could result in some *interesting* consequences!"

At that, she dropped down to lie flat on top of me, throwing her arms around my neck once more, as she leaned in so we were nose to nose. "Then again," she added, "I do love to live dangerously," she purred.

"Oh, you do at that, Max!"

With a laugh, Maxine pulled back to look me straight in the eye. "John Walker, having you for a boyfriend might turn out to be a real pain in the neck for me," she said, her tone warm and loving.

Reaching up to cup her cheek, I smiled. "Doll, I don't think you would want me any other way." I pulled us closer together, brushing her lips with the start of another passionate kiss.

Yep, you guessed it. Max missed her New York flight and had to stay the day, overnight.

Sue me, but I don't think either of us really didn't mind one, single, bit.

END

STEPHEN R. SOBOTKA

TWO OF A KIND

ABOUT THE AUTHOR

Born in the town of Springfield, Missouri and having lived in most of the lower Southeastern States and Oxfordshire, England as part of a Military family, Stephen has cultivated a strong love of reading from an early age. Works of authors such as Tolkien, McCaffrey and Twain have been the catalyst for his growth in imagination and his love of storytelling.

In 1995, he discovered the online community for the animated show *Gargoyles*; through which he developed his talent, and his want for writing 'quality stories'. He remains a fan of the show and is a regular contributor for the annual anthology for the *Gathering of the Gargoyles* convention.

He has written several short stories, featured in such online e-publications as *Twilight Times* and *Sabledrake Magazine*, but "*Two of A Kind*" is his first print publication to date. Stephen plans to continue telling more of John Walker's life in the next "Sin-City Walker" novel, titled "*The Royale Treatment*", which is planned for a 2008-09 release.

Currently he resides in Florida, working on new stories and graphic design work, while maintaining friends in the US, Canada and abroad.

ssobotkajr@gmail.com
http://stephenrsjr.deviantart.com

TWO OF A KIND

STEPHEN R. SOBOTKA